Also by
Kimberly Willis Holt

Novels

My Louisiana Sky
When Zachary Beaver Came to Town
Part of Me: Stories of a Louisiana Family
The Water Seeker

———

The Piper Reed Series
with Christine Davenier

Piper Reed, Navy Brat
Piper Reed, Clubhouse Queen
Piper Reed, Party Planner
Piper Reed, Campfire Girl
Piper Reed, Rodeo Star
Piper Reed, Forever Friend

———

Picture Books

Waiting for Gregory
with Gabi Swiatkowska

Skinny Brown Dog
with Donald Saaf

The Adventures of Granny Clearwater and Little Critter
with Laura Huliska-Beith

Keeper of the Night

Keeper of the Night

KIMBERLY WILLIS HOLT

SQUARE
FISH

HENRY HOLT AND COMPANY
NEW YORK

SQUARE
FISH

An Imprint of Macmillan

Square Fish and the Square Fish logo are trademarks of Macmillan and
are used by Henry Holt and Company under license from Macmillan.

Library of Congress Cataloging-in-Publication Data
Holt, Kimberly Willis. Keeper of the night / Kimberly Willis Holt.
p.   cm.
Summary: Isabel, a thirteen-year-old girl living on the island of Guam,
and her family try to cope with the death of Isabel's mother,
who committed suicide.
[1. Grief—Fiction. 2. Death—Fiction. 3. Family problems—Fiction.
4. Guam—Fiction.] I. Title.
PZ7.H74023 Ke 2003   [Fic]—dc21   2002027553

ISBN 978-0-312-66103-8

Q&A © 2005 by Random House, Inc. Reprinted by permission of Laurel-Leaf, an
imprint of Random House Children's Books, a division of Random House, Inc.

Originally published in the United States by Henry Holt and Company
First Square Fish Edition: September 2011
Square Fish logo designed by Filomena Tuosto
Book designed by Donna Mark
mackids.com

10 9 8 7 6 5 4 3 2 1

AR: 4.4 / LEXILE: 690L

For the people of Guam,
with love and gratitude

Acknowledgments

Writing a book that takes place across the world has its challenges. Thank God for good people. The following people's generosity formed a bridge across a giant ocean and made this story possible: Megan Murphy and her family: John, Austen, Ian, and Sophie Grensbeck; Godfrey and Eugenia Mansapit and their children; Carolyn Merfalen; Christine Scott-Smith; Monica Hopter; Jo Chasse and her 2000 Price Elementary School fifth-grade class; Sherry L. Chargualaf; Herman Crisostomo; David Wiita; Ignacio Cruz; Pat Rankin; Alma Vandervelde; Maureen Murphy and her 2000 Agueda Johnston Middle School summer class.

Manny Crisostomo's excellent publication, *Latte Magazine*, gave me a deeper grasp of many cultural aspects.

Vicki Eder, Director of Amarillo's Suicide and Crisis Center, helped me understand the survivor's view.

Carol Wallace, Kathy Glantz, Cassidy Dill, and Paula Ryan opened their hearts and relived their pain so that I could write an honest book. My story is a better one because they shared theirs.

I once envisioned a day that I would send a manuscript to my editor and agent that had only been read by me. Instead I've discovered I eagerly look forward to the input of the following people:

Shannon Holt, the only person allowed to read my first drafts; Jerry Holt, who actually asked if he could read this one; my talented and loyal friends Jennifer Archer, Charlotte Goebel, and Ronda Thompson.

Thanks to Jean Dayton for graciously typing my manuscript after a virus ate the entire book. And to Adriane Frye for suggesting I rethink a pivotal scene.

My editor, Christy Ottaviano, always challenges me to reach deeper and write another draft. And since I shamelessly seek her approval, I keep reaching. Thanks for loving your craft.

My agent, Jennifer Flannery, cheered me on long before the day she ate carrot sticks at her desk, waiting for the call that would change my life. You are my fairy godmother.

And a special thanks to my parents, Ray and Brenda Willis, who first took me to a magical place called Guam.

Keeper
of the
Night

A Dutiful Daughter

My mother died praying on her knees. Her rosary beads were still in her hands when we found her. She left no note, said no good-byes, gave no last hugs or kisses. Only the empty bottle of sleeping pills that had rolled under her bed proved that she'd meant to leave.

I found her first. But I didn't know she was dead. I thought she was praying.

That morning, I eased her door shut, tied on her apron, and made breakfast for my little brother and sister. I felt proud to scramble their eggs and butter their toast.

Later I tied blue ribbons in Olivia's hair and dipped the comb into a glass of water before parting Frank's. I had no idea it was the first of many mornings I'd be doing that.

Tamuning

After my mother died, my father couldn't bear to look at the front door of our home. I overheard Tata tell my mother's older sister, Auntie Bernadette, that he saw my mother's ghost standing by the door. That's why we're staying with Tata's sister, Auntie Minerva, in Tamuning.

"Just for a little while, Isabel," Tata told me the day we moved here, but it's been five long months. I asked Tata why we couldn't stay with Auntie Bernadette in Malesso. She lives a few houses away from us. But Tata said, "Bernadette is . . . *was* your mother's sister. Not mine."

Tamuning is north of Malesso. Stores and restaurants line the streets. All night long, I lie in bed and smell spicy scents from the Thai restaurant across the road. I hear cars pass on the highway. Sometimes a siren whines, reminding me of the morning the ambulance carried my mother away.

We're stupid staying in Tamuning while our lives take place in Malesso. Everyone we know lives there—

Auntie Bernadette and Uncle Fernando, my friends, our dogs. Our store is there, Frank's school, and my father's boat. We're like clubs trying to be hearts in a stack of cards.

Rides to St. Cletus

*E*ach weekday morning, before the sun rises, Tata slips out of Auntie Minerva's house and heads to Malesso to feed our dogs and spend the day fishing. Later, Auntie Bernadette drives from Malesso to pick us up for school because Auntie Minerva claims she's too busy with the church. Before taking Frank to the public school, Auntie Bernadette drops us off at St. Cletus in Talofofo.

This is Olivia's first year at St. Cletus. She's in second grade, and my father believes when girls get old enough to notice boys, it's good for them to be surrounded by nuns. I'm in eighth grade. The nuns can't stop me from looking.

Auntie Bernadette has no kids of her own and is old enough to be my grandmother. Even though she was born with a crippled hand, she's one of the most respected *suruhanas* on Guam. Auntie heals aches and pains and helps barren women become pregnant. She drives with her right hand, or, as she calls it, her good one. As if the other hand that stays folded, pressed against her chest, is the bad one.

Auntie Bernadette talks the entire way to Talofofo, and in the afternoon she picks us up and talks the entire way back to Auntie Minerva's house.

Olivia likes Auntie's talk because she gets to hear about how Mrs. Cruz's daughter is going to have a baby, but no husband, how Mrs. Santos spent her entire paycheck at bingo, how Roman's mom poured a pitcher of water on Roman's hungover dad and he just rolled over and peed on the couch. Olivia knows more gossip than any seven-year-old at St. Cletus.

One day I tried to remember what my mother said during our daily trips to and from school, but I couldn't remember a single word. My mother lived in a world of her own—a world filled with sadness that I couldn't see.

Sh-sh

My school friends, Delia and Tonya, are back to their normal selves, gossiping about Lola, passing notes in class, sneaking bites of dried squid. But, after my mother died, whenever I approached, one of them would quit talking and say, "Sh-sh."

Even the nuns stopped whispering to each other when I walked by. Sister Agnes nudged Sister Rachel and their bodies straightened. "*Hafa adai,* Isabel."

Sh-sh. So many secrets. Don't they know there's nothing they can tell me about my mother's death?

Unless they know why she left.

Evaporate

Whenever I think of my mother, something fills up inside me, like water filling a bucket. It fills me up so much, I'm afraid my feelings will spill over for everyone to see. So I close my eyes and picture the water in the bucket evaporating until nothing is left, not one single drop.

Monday's List

1. Get up
2. Draw Olivia's bathwater and wake Olivia
3. Hide Olivia's nightgown and wet towels
4. Make sofa bed
5. Get ready for school
6. Remind Frank to comb his hair
7. School
8. Clean bathroom and vacuum
9. Homework
10. Eat dinner
11. Finish homework
12. Read until lights-out

Techa

Auntie Minerva is a *techa*. To be chosen a *techa,* you must know the rosary in Chamorro. Most people my age understand a few Chamorro words like *Hafa adai*, but English is our main language. Even though she lives in Tamuning, Auntie Minerva grew up in Malesso, so she leads the rosary for most of our village's dead. She said the rosary, each of the nine evenings, for my mother.

"I knew the rosary by heart since I was eight," she tells us for the millionth time.

Of course, Auntie Minerva doesn't perform the rosary every day, but she finds reasons to go to church. Usually to light a candle and pray for someone. Tonight she lifts her muumuu and shows me the bruises on her knobby knees. "This afternoon I prayed for six hours straight," she says. "But my suffering is nothing like our Savior's."

When Auntie Minerva isn't fasting, she barely eats. Twice I caught her spitting food into a napkin; she's afraid to put some meat on those bones. I've seen the way she shakes her head, studying Auntie Bernadette's full hips.

It's been almost six months since we came to Auntie Minerva's house. Every couple of weeks I ask Tata when we will go home.

"Soon," he always says. But he never looks in my eyes when he says it.

After Auntie Minerva's tasteless dinner tonight, I ask Tata again. And when he answers the same thing, I tell him, "You always say that. Are we going to live here forever? Why can't we go home?"

Tata glares at me. "We will go when I say so."

I should know better. Tata always does as he pleases, never minding anyone else's feelings. When I was younger, I pretended I wanted to fish so I could be near him, but he never asked me along. And when he returned from the sea, he claimed he was tired. He was never too tired to drink beer in the cabana with his friends almost every night. Frank was the one he spent time with, but that changed when Frank became afraid of the water.

Back then I liked going to Mass because he went, too, and we sat on the pew together like a real family. But Tata hasn't been to Mass since my mother died.

Sometimes I get angry when I watch television programs that show fathers who take their kids to the movies, play basketball with them in driveways, and give great advice. I don't know any dads like that.

Smart Boy

Frank would rather do my math homework than show me how to work the problems. "I don't understand," I tell him when he works out my algebra without any trouble.

"What don't you understand?" he asks.

"If I knew, I'd tell you."

He shrugs, then lowers his head and tackles the next problem. After he's done, he pushes the paper toward me. "See?"

I shake my head.

He sighs, taking back my assignment. His pencil meets the paper and he doesn't stop until he finishes my homework. I don't object. I'll just make sure that I erase some of the right answers and replace them with wrong ones. Sister Agnes would never believe I aced my algebra. But would she believe me if I said my seventh-grade brother did it for me? Frank hasn't even covered variables. He's taking pre-algebra this year. It doesn't seem fair that Frank got all the smart genes in the family.

House of Plastic

Auntie Minerva's house may be made from concrete brick, but inside it's plastic—plastic on her furniture, plastic Tupperware in her cabinets, plastic smile on her face.

Today Olivia's foot accidentally brushes the coffee table.

Auntie Minerva gives her a stiff smile. "Olivia, you must be careful with the blessings God has given us."

"Did God give Olivia that coffee table?" I ask.

Auntie Minerva shoots me a sharp look and her lips purse. Then her mouth slides into that plastic grin. "Isabel, don't you have homework?"

"No," I say.

"Then read Leviticus 19:32. Maybe you will learn something new about how to speak to your elders, especially those who, out of the goodness of their hearts, take you under their roof and put food in your belly."

Auntie Minerva is a terrible cook. When I tell Auntie Bernadette this, she says, "That's because Minerva doesn't like to eat." Auntie Bernadette has a magnet on her refrigerator that says never trust a skinny cook.

Sneaky

Frank shares the guest bedroom with Tata while Olivia and I share the sofa sleeper in the living room. We sleep with two folded towels beneath us because the night my mother died, Olivia wet the bed. She hasn't had a dry night since. In the mornings I rise before anyone in the house. I hide the wet towels and Olivia's nightgown in a sack inside my book bag, fill the bathtub for Olivia, and fold the couch into place.

Auntie Bernadette and I are like spies on a secret mission. She takes the towels and Olivia's nightgown home and washes them, then gives them back to me after school. Auntie Minerva is always at church when I get home, so I can slip the towels between the sheets before she returns.

Olivia never looks at the wet towels in the morning or the clean ones Auntie Bernadette hands to me every afternoon. Maybe she's pretending nothing ever happened.

Lunchtime at St. Cletus

Fish stew day.
Sit with Delia and Tonya day.
Eat sour mangoes and hot sauce day.
Pass notes in class day.
Tell secrets about naughty Lola and the boys day.
Nothing's changed.

A Meal of Words

Frank hasn't made any friends in Tamuning. After school, he does his homework at the kitchen table. He's smart and makes the honor roll every year but hates to read. I love to read, but I haven't been on the honor roll since third grade.

Today I sit across from him, trying to study for my science test. I reread the same page three times, but the words won't sink in. I don't like to read just anything. "You'd make straight As," Tata says, "if they gave a quiz on romance." I read love stories. I've read hundreds. I like happy endings.

Frank writes tiny letters in his notebook. I try to read them upside down. When he catches me looking at his notebook, he tears the paper away from the spiral and rips it into thin strips, wads them into pea-sized balls, and pops them in his mouth. He swallows each bite and frowns at me. After every word disappears through his mouth, every sentence slides to his gut, he announces, "Delicious!"

Wanted:
One Knock-Knock Joke

Once Auntie Bernadette asked Frank why he was so quiet. Frank looked at her a long moment and said, "I'll tell you when I have something to say." He was eight when he said that and I remember thinking what a weird thing for a little boy to say. But Auntie said, "Frank, you are an old soul."

When he did speak, he told a lot of knock-knock jokes.

"Isabel, knock, knock."

"Who's there?"

"Knock, knock."

"Who's there?"

"Knock, knock."

Sigh. "Who's there?"

"Orange."

"Orange who?"

"Orange you glad I didn't say knock, knock?"

Mom would laugh, but I got so sick of his jokes I wanted to yank every hair out of his head.

Now I'd give anything to hear one more corny knock-knock joke.

Magic Man

Every morning Tata leaves before we awake. He doesn't return until we've finished our supper. Olivia meets him at the door and gives him a hug. I wait to see if he'll hug me, but he never does.

He eats his dinner with a Miller Lite. "How's school?" he asks on the way to bed but doesn't stop to hear my answer. He slips into the guest room and closes the door. He's the magic man, reinventing the disappearing act.

Dishes

Tonight, Auntie Minerva takes her religious plates off the wall and places them by the dinner dishes I'm washing. "You might as well wash these, too," she says, placing the plate of Jesus holding a lamb on top. "They're very dusty."

I fill the sink with fresh water and soap. I hold my breath as I dip the plate under the suds and say a little prayer that I don't break Auntie Minerva's precious plates.

Auntie Minerva surprises me by picking up a cloth and drying the plates. "You know, Isabel, you need to watch out because you look just like your mother."

I should have known she had a reason for helping me with the dishes.

"Yes, you'll have to be careful. You have those light brown eyes and thick dark hair just like her. Beauty can make life seem easy at first, but it can cause trouble later. Your mother had things too easy in life."

The Lord's Supper plate is in my hands and it's very tempting to drop it on the floor, but I carefully hand it to her and grab the next. An hour later, Auntie Minerva's words play over and over in my mind. I know she's wrong. My mother's beauty didn't cause life to be easy for her. No one leaves an easy life behind. But now Auntie Minerva's comments make me think about how I do look like my mother. Maybe that's why Tata ignores me.

Delia's New Haircut

Delia has a new short haircut, "a shaggy bob," she calls it. Just like the girl on the cover of *Seventeen* magazine. Today the boys seem to notice her, or maybe they notice how she now stands tall and walks like she owns the island. Maybe they like the Barely Rose lip gloss she paints on her mouth. Yesterday Delia wore her shoulders for earrings, shuffled her feet as she moved across the floor, and used cherry-flavored Chap Stick.

"Maybe I'll go to modeling school," she tells Tonya and me.

Tonya sucks in her plump tummy.

"Maybe you should pass math first," I say.

"Humph. Who needs math to model?"

I wink at Tonya, then ask Delia, "How will you count all that big money you're going to make?"

Sister Agnes and
Sister Rachel

Sister Agnes doesn't look like her name. She is beautiful—smooth creamy brown skin, high cheekbones, large dark eyes. Her long eyelashes need no mascara, which is a good thing since sisters can't wear makeup.

She teaches us science and math. "Don't you see?" she asks us. "There is science everywhere. In your body, at the beach, the salamander running across your windowsill."

She tries to make the most boring subject fascinating. She flaps her arms and imitates cell reproduction. But when she talks, I try to picture what her hair might look like cut into a short shaggy bob. And how would her lips look wearing Barely Rose lip gloss? Did she have a boyfriend when she was my age?

Sister Rachel is another matter. She teaches English and social studies. Her woolly brows meet over her nose and her upper lip needs waxing. She must have planned to be a nun from the day she was born.

List Maker

"What are you doing?" my mother would ask when she saw me writing in my notebook. "Lists again?" She'd roll her eyes. "You're too young to have to cross things off a list. You worry too much."

But I kept writing. Someone had to remember to do things.

My Mother's Gifts

Olivia makes Auntie Minerva nervous because she never sits still. She dances, skips, twirls. She reminds me of the next-door lady's Australian terrier searching for a place to poop. I try to keep an eye on her so that Auntie Minerva doesn't snap at us and complain to our father.

When he's not doing homework, Frank plays that Korean game *kong-gi* or marbles. When my mother was alive, she taught Frank to play her ukulele. He made up songs and sang them. He has a beautiful voice and last year was chosen to sing a solo in his school choir concert. He's like my mother in that way, as Olivia is like her with her dancing. They have my mother's gifts.

Though after my mother died, the songs in Frank's head dried up and his fingers held *kong-gi* pieces instead of strumming the strings of her ukulele.

Olivia didn't change. She dances and giggles so much,

sometimes I want to say, "Don't you remember? Our mother died."

I may look like my mother, but I'm not like her. I don't like to dance or sing. I don't like to pray. I'm not like my mother at all. I am here.

A Charitable Act

Auntie Minerva believes we should earn our keep. Olivia must dust and I'm in charge of cleaning the bathroom and kitchen.

Frank mows twice a week and weeds the flower beds. The first day, he not only mowed Auntie Minerva's yard, he mowed her neighbors' yards on both sides of her house.

"What a good boy!" the neighbors said when they saw Frank had included their yards.

Auntie Minerva smiled smugly and said, "Good raising," as if she'd given birth to Frank and taught him everything he knew.

I was impressed, too. Frank didn't usually do what he was asked, much less more. The second time Frank mowed, I watched him from the kitchen window. His eyes glazed, he seemed so far away. If the sidewalks weren't there to stop his path, I think he would have mowed the entire street.

The lazy neighbors didn't bother mowing the next week, but that was the last time Frank mowed their lawns.

"Too much gas wasted," Auntie Minerva declared. Now she has to nag Frank to start the engine.

List of Confessions

Forgive me, Father, for I have sinned.

1. Forgive me for sneaking the wet towels behind Auntie Minerva's back.
2. Forgive me for yelling at Olivia when she didn't dust the coffee table.
3. Forgive me for being jealous of Delia's haircut.
4. Forgive me for not doing my homework last Wednesday, Thursday, and Friday.
5. Forgive me for lying to my friends about having my period.
6. Forgive me for getting impatient with Tata.
7. Forgive me for once wishing that my mother was dead.

Marking Time

It might be easier to notice the passing of time if I lived in Maine. When winter came, there would be snow. When spring arrived, I'd fly a kite. In the summer, birds would sing for their breakfast, and in the autumn, leaves would turn crimson and fall.

But I live on an island where every day is almost the same as the day before and the day after. The temperature stays hot. The trees are always green. The birds don't visit us here, unless you count the chickens. Even the dry season isn't so different from the rainy season. And each day that passes doesn't seem to get me any closer to home.

Things to Do That Might
Help Us Return to Malesso

1. Make my father proud of me.
   A. Don't argue with Auntie Minerva (even if she snaps at Olivia).
   B. Go to Mass with Auntie Minerva.
   C. Keep Auntie Minerva's house clean.
   D. Take Olivia to the bathroom in the middle of the night so she won't wet the bed.
   E. Try, try, try to make Bs in every class (except maybe science; a C in science would be okay).
2. Pray that my mother's ghost will leave our house.

Teacher for the Day

$\mathcal{A}$ sociology class at the university wants to interview Auntie Bernadette about her life as a *suruhana*.

"Come with me," she says. "It will get you away from Minerva for the afternoon."

Auntie loves being in front of the classroom. She likes all eyes on her. She likes answering the students' questions.

"How do you explain your power to heal?" they want to know.

"My heavenly Father gave the gift to me," she says. "I was born feet first. Babies born feet first have the healing touch."

Some nod like they believe that's true, too. Others say "Oh." Now they understand.

"Why do you use spoons to massage?"

"My mother used the spoons." She says this as if that alone is enough.

A girl raises her hand and Auntie points her way. "Yes?"

"Is it difficult to work with your handicap?" the girl asks, and sinks lower into her seat.

Auntie smiles. "I don't know any other way. God took one thing but gave me another."

The girl nods, looking relieved.

"What is the strangest thing someone wanted you to do?"

"I can't say that with my young niece here." Now all eyes turn toward me.

"But," Auntie says loudly, and they're back in her trance. "I told him I'm not that kind of woman. And that's not the kind of healing I do."

The students and the teacher laugh. I don't, but I know why they're laughing. I'm not that young.

After class, the teacher asks Auntie Bernadette to stay for the next one.

Auntie smiles. "You're lucky. I don't have any appointments this afternoon."

I sigh, not meaning to be heard, but the teacher and Auntie Bernadette notice.

"Isabel," the teacher says, "would you like to walk around the campus while your auntie talks to my next class? You could watch the diving team at the pool. They're champions this year."

"Thank you, miss," I say as I slip out the door and head across the campus grounds.

Falling into Water

No one notices me at the swimming pool. They're watching the man on the high diving board. He wears a red Speedo and his head is clean shaven like most of the other divers'. He pauses a moment, then stretches his arms above his head and bends at the waist. With a bounce, he dives. But before he reaches the pool, he turns into a ball and spins in the air. Then his body unfolds and becomes a straight arrow pointing toward the water. His arms break the surface and lead the way. After he swims to the edge of the pool, the next diver takes his place. And the dance begins again.

I want to know how that feels.

Phone Call

I miss my friends in Malesso. My father sees Roman almost every day and tells me his fishing stories. But I'm curious about Teresita. Is she still winning cockfights? I even miss Mrs. Cruz, the fish artist, and the hot-dog lady, who sells hot dogs and slices of green papaya from her stand at the pier.

Each village celebrates its patron saint with a fiesta every year. Malesso's saint is San Dimas. I wonder if we'll return before fiesta time.

I pick up the phone to call Teresita even though I should know better. Teresita isn't like Tonya or Delia. She hates talking on the phone. Sometimes Delia and I just breathe into the receiver while we watch the same TV show.

Teresita answers and I say, "Teresita, how is Malesso?"

"It's still here." Silence. Then Teresita says, "But you're not. I miss you, girl."

Teresita's remark both pleases and surprises me. She always acts so tough. But I think that's because she's had to be. Her mother is addicted to ice. Some people call it "poor man's cocaine" because it's cheap to make. Tata says cheap to make, expensive to get off. He says it steals people's lives. All I know is that it stole Teresita's mom from her.

No Crying Over Spilled Milk

Olivia spins and spins around the living room and knocks over Frank's cherry Kool-Aid. On my knees, I press paper towels into the red spot on the beige carpet.

"Hurry, hurry, Isabel," Olivia cries, tearing more paper from the roll. My heart pounds fast as I try to make the stain disappear before Auntie Minerva returns from church. Frank is stretched out on the couch, staring at the spot.

"Frank, don't just sit there," I yell. He picks up the glass and takes it into the kitchen.

I'm on my seventh paper towel when Auntie Minerva opens the front door ten minutes early.

She sees the red stain and doesn't even ask who. Olivia's whimper gives her away. Auntie Minerva grabs her and shakes her like a rag doll.

"Stop!" I yell, pulling my sister from her. Auntie Minerva falls off balance and slides against the back of her plastic-covered couch until she reaches the floor. She lands with her legs spread wide, her hair loose from her tight bun. On the floor, rosary beads peek out from her purse.

Frank starts out of the kitchen, but when he sees Auntie, he freezes in the doorway.

"You children are ungrateful and ill-mannered," Auntie Minerva says. "Wait until your father sees what you've done. Wait until he hears." She narrows her eyes at me.

That night I don't need to ask Tata when we will go home. Olivia asks instead.

"This Friday, after school," he says. Then he pats her on the head and whispers, "Don't cry over spilled milk."

If I'd known all it would have taken was to spill cherry Kool-Aid on Auntie Minerva's carpet, I'd have done it months ago. I'd have made a red trail from the front door of her living room through the back door of her kitchen.

"You must apologize to your auntie," Tata tells me. My father is old-fashioned, with old-fashioned ways. That's why I call him Tata while my friends call their fathers Dad. He's from the old world. The world where young people tell their elders they're sorry even when their elders are wrong.

So before bed, I say, "I'm sorry, Auntie Minerva, for being disrespectful." My lips and tongue say the words while I decide if I'll pack my underwear or my dresses first.

Return to Malesso

Today we leave Tamuning and return to our home in Malesso. Auntie Minerva kisses our cheeks before we hop into Tata's truck.

"Remember your prayers," she says. "Count your blessings each night."

Tata offers her a fifty-dollar bill. She shakes her head and pushes his hand away. Tata holds the money out in front of her, but Auntie Minerva keeps protesting. Then as he starts to return it to his wallet, she snatches it. "I'll give the money to the church and I'll light a candle for you."

Auntie Minerva's hands grip my shoulders. "Isabel, you are the woman of the house now, the only mother Frank and Olivia will probably remember. Shameful to say."

I wiggle loose and hurry to the truck before she erases my mother completely.

"I'll miss you," Auntie Minerva calls out to us.

I won't miss the long prayers said before each meal and bedtime, her dry chicken *kelaguen,* or the plastic-covered furniture sticking to my legs.

Malesso

€very year the newspaper sponsors a contest and the people vote for the most beautiful village on Guam. The southern villages almost always win and Malesso wins most often.

We have no hotels or big stores or busy intersections. Here purple bougainvilleas grow as tall as trees. Pink and white chain of love vines embrace the flame trees along the road that travels aside a turquoise sea. The bell tower overlooks the ocean and Cocos Island near the horizon. I didn't see any of this until today.

Today I notice the bougainvilleas, the chain of love vines, the turquoise sea, the bell tower as if discovering them for the first time. Did my mother ever see them?

Home

We arrive at our home—the blue cement house I've lived in since the day I was born. Our tiny store, next to our home, looks like a haunted house with boards nailed over the windows.

Tata walks through our front door, where he saw my mother's ghost. It doesn't seem to faze him. Maybe Tata practiced coming home after fishing every day. Maybe he took tiny steps, each day walking closer until he could turn the knob. But now I watch how he moves fast through the house with his suitcase and doesn't even unpack—just heads outside again. He grabs his net and walks across the street toward the ocean.

As he leaves, Tata tells me to flip the sign hanging on the door of our store that said CLOSED for the past six months. That means I'm the one who must wait for customers in the cabana. Who will want six-month-old bread, rotten pickled eggs, and freezer-burned Häagen-Dazs ice cream? I decide to make a list for the vendors.

Tata built the cabana from bamboo and banana plant leaves. A coconut tree bends over it and after Olivia had a close call with a coconut, my father attached a net underneath to catch any falling fruit.

From the picnic table, I watch Tata's back until his short body could be any of the village men. But when he throws the net, anyone would know it was Tata. Only a fine fisherman throws a net in the air in such a way that it lands on the water in a perfect circle. When he gathers up the net, I rush inside the house to unpack my clothes.

Frank has already unpacked and is heading outside, *kong-gi* pieces in hand. Olivia plays in the backyard with the dogs. Her bag of clothes is in the middle of the hall.

"Come here, Olivia," I say, "You need to unpack."

"You're not my mother," she tells me.

I dump her clothes on the floor, thinking, Yes, you're right. I'm not.

List for Vendors

50 cans of Spam

20 pints of Häagen-Dazs ice cream

15 dozen eggs

12 gallons of milk

10 boxes of various candies

1 case of Coca-Cola

1 case of Diet Coke

1 case of 7UP

1 case of Dr Pepper

4 cases of Miller Lite

4 cases of Bud Light

5 gallons of *tuba* (buy from Roman's dad)

Betel nuts

A Place at the Table

While I was in Tamuning, it was as if what happened to my mother didn't happen. It was as if we were away on a trip and she was waiting on the other end of the island. But now the house is filled with her—the room where she died, her zoris by the front door, her ukulele. Everywhere I go, I bump into my mother's ghost.

At dinner, her chair is empty, the chair she chose so she could see the ocean from the window as she ate. Olivia stares at my mother's seat, then quickly squeezes her eyes together, like she does when I clean her scraped knees with alcohol.

"Let's trade places," I say.

"Like musical chairs?" she asks.

"Sort of. But we won't take any chairs away."

Tata is still fishing, but Frank, Olivia, and I lift our plates and swap seats. I sit in Olivia's chair. Olivia sits in mine. Frank takes Tata's. No one chooses our mother's.

Olivia thinks trading places is a game. But Frank and I look at each other and quickly glance away.

I'll never have one special place at the table. I'll sit in a different place every day. Then if I go away, no one will miss me just by looking at an empty chair.

My Room

In a special room I have a four-poster bed with an ivory bedspread and lacy pillows at the headboard. A yellow desk is in the corner. There my secret journal is locked in a drawer with a key I wear around my neck. The journal knows my secrets.

There's also a lock on my door. No one can come in without knocking first. Not even Olivia. That is the special room of my dreams.

I share my real room with Olivia. I don't keep a journal because I don't have a yellow desk with a lock on the drawer. I do have a nosy little sister who likes to tell secrets.

We have twin beds, no headboards, just mattresses on top of box springs on top of metal bed frames. Most nights our beds stay against opposite walls. During typhoons, we push our beds together in the middle of the room. Some nights we push them together and I hold

Olivia and tell her stories about talking pigs that wear sunglasses and drive sports cars.

Tonight there are no typhoons or any new stories in my head about talking pigs. But we push our beds together anyway.

First Night

Olivia wakes twice from nightmares.
Two trips to the bathroom.
I don't sleep at all.

First Morning List

1. Dress
2. Make bed
3. Make my father's bed
4. Make breakfast for my family
5. Brush teeth
6. Fix Olivia's hair
7. Sit in cabana and wait for customers

First Morning Home

1. Dress—My clothes aren't in the drawer. Olivia has shoved them under the bed next to deserted gecko eggs.
2. Make bed—Olivia won't get out of bed so that I can make it.
3. Make Tata's bed—His bed is already made. He's never made a bed in his life, not even at Auntie Minerva's.
4. Make breakfast for my family—Tata says, "I'm not hungry," as he leaves for his boat. Olivia refuses to eat my "mushy" pancakes.

   "I like mushy pancakes," Frank says, and gobbles down his tall stack.
5. Brush teeth—My toothbrush tastes like toilet water, stinky pee flavor. Olivia giggles outside the bathroom door.

6. Fix Olivia's hair—I don't even try to comb out her tangles.
7. Sit in the cabana and wait for customers—I can always count on some things to go as planned.

No-Legend Death

"Your mother would have been proud," says Auntie Bernadette, "if she knew you could make the *golai hagun sune*. Why don't you make it for her first anniversary rosary?"

Six months ago no one worried about what would make my mother proud.

"Erlinda will be lucky to have a church burial," Auntie Minerva had told my father then. Not long ago, people who committed suicide didn't get a rosary or a funeral blessed by the church.

But Auntie Minerva was wrong. No one questioned giving my mother a proper burial. No one questioned or said anything about the way she died. At least not around us. Every night of the nine-day rosary my family wore the same thing—our best clothes and shoes and a coat of shame.

On Guam there's a legend about two lovers. It's an old story, hundreds of years old. Everyone on our island has heard the legend. Two young people in love hoped to marry. But the girl's father, a head chief, forbade the union because he had promised her to a Spanish captain.

Not willing to live without each other, the two young lovers climbed to one of the highest cliffs on the island, tied their long hair together, and leaped to their death.

A giant monument stands there now—two bodies intertwined. They call the place Two Lovers Point. People visit the statue and pay homage to true love.

No one built a monument for my mother's death. Only looks of pity are left, like the shells that remain on the beach after the tide leaves.

I don't want to make the *golai hagun sune*.

Cocos Island

After school I used to sit in the cabana with my mother and she'd braid my hair while we waited for customers. She'd laugh when I told her something silly—like when Sister Agnes tried to juggle guavas, then fell after slipping on a dropped fruit. Those days my mother smelled like chicken *kelaguen* or fried fish or whatever she cooked for dinner.

Even on my mother's quiet days, her fingers laced sections of my hair together with ease as she stared out at the waves. Those days she smelled like salt from the ocean and I knew that Auntie Bernadette would bring us supper.

Now I must take my mother's place, sitting in the cabana alone.

It's Saturday morning and the tour buses from Tumon come to Malesso. Their loud engines rattle our windows as they pass us by. We smell their diesel long after they leave. Before the buses started coming, the Japanese tourists drove rental cars through our village and often stopped at our store for a Coke or Häagen-Dazs ice cream. Now they buy at the larger store on the pier.

Then they load onto the boat for the ten-minute ride to Cocos Island. They will swim, ride Jet Skis, or parasail for the day. If they have big bucks, they might stay at the fancy hotel for a night or two. I've only been to Cocos Island once. Years ago, when Olivia was a baby. Tata took Frank and me for the day. But when we returned, my mother was curled up in bed and Olivia was crying, her diapers soaked and heavy with poop. We never went back after that.

Tata said he liked Cocos Island better before they made it a resort. He said the island used to have cabins, and when they were newlyweds he and my mother often rode out in his boat and spent the night there. I don't see much difference, one island from the next. Besides, Cocos Island is only a mile away and not much bigger than a tiny village.

Mrs. Camacho, who lives down the road, used to complain to her husband that he never took her anywhere. She was born and raised on Guam and had never been off island. On their twenty-fifth anniversary Mr. Camacho told her he would surprise her and take her away. She was so excited. Auntie Bernadette said she packed and unpacked for a week. "What if it's cold?" she asked Auntie Bernadette. "What if I need a coat?"

Mrs. Camacho shouldn't have worried. Where did her husband take her? Cocos Island.

Roman

"How are you doing, old friend?" Roman asks me like he's really interested in what happened while I was away from Malesso. He doesn't fool me. He's wondering where my father is.

Roman thinks Tata strung up the moon and stars in the sky. "Your father is the greatest fisherman on the island. He knows the best places to catch the biggest skipjack and he gets more crab than anyone in Malesso." He tells me this like I'm not my father's daughter. Like I'm some dumb girl who has never scraped out the guts of a fish.

Roman's parents have known mine since they were children. When Roman and I were little, they teased us that we'd marry one day. I don't plan to marry a boy with a crooked grin, who smells like fish, a boy who dreams of catching the biggest skipjack in the ocean or the most crab on full-moon nights.

Roman attends the public junior high school with Teresita in Inarajan. It's not cheap to go to my school, St. Cletus, but my father is a good fisherman. Roman's father isn't. He's not good at much of anything except making *tuba* and drinking too much beer.

When Roman isn't fishing, he practices casting his rod in the front yard, repairs his net, or helps his mother. Tata says Roman is righting the lazy ways of his father.

Teresita

Hours go by and not one customer; only Roman and Auntie Bernadette visit me in the cabana.

Teresita hasn't stopped by yet, but I should know, the chickens come first. She wants to be the best cockfighter on the island, more famous than Lorenzo, king of the cockfighters. She lives with her auntie and uncle and helps her uncle with his chickens, training and feeding them.

Around three o'clock, Teresita arrives and I feel a warmth surround me like a blanket on a cool night. It's the way I felt yesterday when I returned to Malesso.

Teresita's hands roll into fists. Her jaw locked, she paces back and forth like her chickens. "That stupid uncle of mine! He lost more money last night at the Dededo dome. He never closes the pen when his chickens fight."

Teresita shakes her head when she tells me this. She believes when someone's chicken fights, he is guaranteed to lose if he doesn't close the cage door. She also believes people shouldn't sleep, eat, or sweep around the chickens at a cockfight.

Teresita is superstitious, but maybe she knows what she's talking about because her chickens always win when she challenges the boys to secret fights. It's illegal to have cockfights without a license. Even the mayor must get permission from the governor to hold them during fiesta. Once he forgot and Tata said there was hell to pay.

Teresita acts like she could not care less that her mother is addicted to ice and lives in another village with a boyfriend. Her long black hair sweeps the ground as she walks. The boys used to pull her hair when we were younger. Now the boys tell Teresita how pretty her hair is and ask her to promise to never cut it. That's why most days Teresita wears her hair in a ponytail or twists it into a bun on top of her head. Except during cock-fights with the boys. She always wears her hair down then.

Not once does Teresita say, "Isabel, it's good to have you back home." Or, "How did you keep from going crazy at your cranky old auntie's house?" It's as if she forgot I ever left. That's okay, though. Teresita makes the sun sink fast and before I know it, Tata will return with fish and I can close the store.

Lorenzo,
King of the Cockfighters

Tata returns home early, a couple of hours before the sun sets. He says it's okay if I go with Teresita to buy a hot dog down at the pier.

On the way, we stop at Teresita's pink house for her CD player. Then we walk along, our heads bobbing to the beat of Eminem.

I'm slim shady, yes, I'm the real shady . . .

At Lorenzo's house three workmen carry a hot tub toward his front door. Lorenzo follows close behind, his arms waving in the air. "Careful, careful," he tells them. "Do you know how much money that cost me?"

Last year, Lorenzo put a swimming pool in his backyard. The swimming pool stretches beyond the sides of his tiny house. It has a diving board. Lorenzo doesn't even swim in it. About a hundred chicken pens dot his yard. Those chickens paid for the swimming pool and the hot tub.

Lorenzo bought his chickens with money he earned sewing up prized ones at the cockfights. People pay a lot of bucks to squeeze a few more games out of a winning chicken.

Teresita learned to sew up the chickens from Lorenzo. He didn't offer to teach her. She watched. Lorenzo claims she stole from him because now a lot of people run outside the dome with their chickens for Teresita to fix instead of waiting in Lorenzo's line. Costs them half as much, too. Teresita sews them up in the parking lot because she's too young to be inside. Before she started her side business, she watched the fights inside the dome and no one said anything. But now Lorenzo watches with snake eyes, ready to tell the authorities if Teresita sets a toe inside the dome.

I'm slim shady, I'm the real shady . . .

Teresita and I slide right on by Lorenzo's house. We don't even say hey.

The Fish Artist

Teresita and I eat our hot dogs and sour papaya at the pier. Mrs. Cruz, the fish artist, sits surrounded by her paintings while she waits for the tourists. Her huge thighs pour over the lawn chair. If she stood quickly, the chair would stick to her behind like the shell on a tortoise's back.

"*Hafa adai*, Isabel. Did you hear? I'm going to be a grandmother."

"Yes, congratulations."

"You've grown so much since I've seen you last. You're pretty enough to be fiesta queen."

Teresita snickers. We've spent many afternoons making fun of the fiesta queen pageant.

"Thank you," I say, "but no, not me."

"Your mother was Malesso's prettiest fiesta queen." I don't say a word, but I don't have to. The boat is pulling up to dock and Mrs. Cruz stands up, ready for action. Amazingly, the chair stays in place.

You're not supposed to sell things to the tourists on the pier, but no one says anything to Mrs. Cruz. Her paintings are the way she feeds her pregnant daughter and son, John Wayne, since her husband left them for another woman—Mrs. Cruz's sister—and escaped to her island, Palau.

People talked that it was because of their son that Mr. Cruz left. John Wayne is not right in the head. His face looks like a pug dog's—he has a flat nose and his eyes are wide apart. He's thirteen, the same age as me, but he acts like a five-year-old. Roman says even though John Wayne is mentally retarded, he's one of the smartest people he knows. "Never mind that John Wayne can't read or write," he says. "He's a great spear fisherman."

John Wayne's real name is Wayne. But he loves cow-boys and wears a cowboy hat every day. Everyone calls him John Wayne, even his mom, who would call him Hercules if he wanted her to.

My father said when John Wayne was six, he took to spear fishing like other kids take to playing Nintendo. Back then, Mrs. Cruz used to paint other things besides fish. She painted Cocos Island, sunsets, nude people, but never fish.

Mrs. Cruz tried to teach her son to kill only the fish they'd eat. But John Wayne couldn't resist. He'd spear any fish he saw.

So Mrs. Cruz put away all the things in her head that she wanted to paint and instead painted skipjack, tuna, and atlulai. "See the pretty fish," she'd say. "Don't kill all the pretty fish. Leave some for us to admire, some for me to paint."

It didn't work. John Wayne gets a big thrill out of the fish he stabs. He holds up his spear for everyone to see and dances around in a circle. "See what I did!" he sings, while the fish flops on his spear. "See, see, I got a fish!" It doesn't matter if he catches another one in five minutes. Spear held high overhead, he dances and sings the same words.

One good thing came out of Mrs. Cruz's plan. Her fish paintings are very popular with the tourists. I guess no one wants a picture of a naked lady, but everyone is proud to hang a fish on their wall.

The Way It Was Before

Frank is in the cabana, playing *kong-gi*. I wonder why he's not with his friends. Isn't he glad to be home? Doesn't he want life to go back to the way it was before?

Back then, Frank's friends hung out in the cabana after school and on Saturdays. Frank played the ukulele or, if it was a good day, my mother played. The boys were in love with her, but not as much as Frank. Not like my father loved her, but a love, I guess, that a boy has for his mother. And a love that she has for him. It was different with Olivia and me. My mother looked at Frank like he had wings and could fly across the ocean. When he first began to play the ukulele, Mom covered her mouth and cried tears of joy. When Olivia danced, she'd beg my mother to watch her, but Mom would narrow her eyes and rub her temples as if it gave her a headache to see Olivia cha-cha. I hated my mother in those moments when she wouldn't pretend to be happy.

Auntie Bernadette walks toward our house, carrying

a sack filled with our dinner. I'd forgotten the time because my stomach is still full from the hot dog and papaya. Maybe Frank's friends were here earlier but had to leave for supper. I think my mother was right. I worry too much.

Second Night

Tonight when Olivia cries out "No!" in her sleep, I gently wake her. "It's only a bad dream, little sister."

Why didn't the nightmares start at Auntie Minerva's house, where my auntie's laws made life difficult?

I hold Olivia until she finishes crying. She buries her face in my chest. "I'm sorry, Isabel."

Sorry for what? Sorry for waking me? Or sorry for hiding my clothes under the bed, not eating my mushy pancakes, or dipping my toothbrush in the toilet?

One good thing has come because of the nightmares—dry sheets. Before Olivia falls back to sleep, I take her to the bathroom, tuck her into bed, and walk softly to the kitchen for a glass of water. My father's bedroom door is ajar and I learn why his bed was made this morning.

He's asleep on the floor, his body curled in the exact same spot where my mother took her last breath.

Sleepy Days,
Sleepless Nights

Sister Agnes called my name several times in class before I answered her. At least that's what Tonya tells me at lunch. "Your eyes are red, Isabel. Are you all right?"

"I'm sleepy," I say.

At night, I try not to look at the clock because then I know how much time I have left before I must get ready for school. But the white numbers draw me to them like a magnet, and I spend most of the night watching the numbers flip into new ones. I wish I could go to sleep after Olivia's nightmare and trip to the bathroom, but thoughts keep my mind racing. There's so much to think about. Thank goodness I have my lists to keep it all straight.

Lost Birds

My mother told me that, years ago, Guam had many birds—beautiful birds with beautiful songs. But the brown tree snake took over the island, eating the bird eggs until one day there weren't any birds left. An occasional sparrow may find its way here, but that's about it.

"Only chickens crowing all hours of the day, crowing like broken alarm clocks," Mom said, her eyes growing wet like someone crying over their dead dog. Since I didn't remember the birds, I never understood her tears.

But now I long for the birds like she did. A hole inside me waits to be filled with their melodies. I toss and turn at night. I want to hear the birds' songs and see them spread their wings. Then maybe I could fly away with them.

Golai Hagun Sune

Auntie Bernadette won't quit nagging me about the *golai hagun sune*. Her words are like pebbles hitting my head. "You should let me show you how to make it for the fiesta. Then you'll have some practice before your mother's first anniversary rosary."

I don't tell Auntie that I already know how to make the *golai hagun sune*. I watched my mother make it for years, just as she watched her mother. I saw how she slowly rubbed the coconut meat against the grinder, squeezing it to capture every drop. So much work for so little milk. I followed her into the backyard as she picked the best taro leaves; only the flawless ones went into her dish.

"Anything that takes this long," she'd say, "is made with love." I remember thinking, Anything that takes this long is not worth making.

Everyone raved about my mother's *golai hagun sune*.

"So sweet!"

"So smooth!"

Golai hagun sune was Frank's favorite dish. He'd rather eat it than pizza.

The other women in our family stopped making *golai hagun sune* for fiestas, rosaries, or even for their husbands. "We can't compete with Erlinda's," they'd say. "She's the gifted one." I believe they were the clever ones, finding a way to stop making it.

Every day, Auntie Bernadette reminds me, "Fiesta will be here soon. You better learn now. It's not an easy dish."

Mary Kelly

The new girl at school is blond, blue-eyed, with skin as pale as coconut meat—a real haole. She stands in front of the class, holding her fat mother's hand like a little girl who doesn't want to be left alone in a room full of darkies like us.

Sister Luke smiles and puts her arm around the girl's shoulders. "Class, this is Mary Kelly Johnson. She's a new student here at St. Cletus. Let's welcome her."

"*Hafa adai*, Mary Kelly," we say together on key. The boys begin their eyebrow talk. They really want to welcome her—show her the island ways.

Her mother leaves and Mary Kelly looks like she's going to cry, standing there in front of our class. Big haole crybaby. Why doesn't she go to her own school on the navy base?

Eyebrow Talk

The men and boys on Guam have a language all their own—no words are spoken. It's the eyebrow talk.

When a guy likes a girl, he moves his eyebrows up and down two or three times. That says, You're pretty, you're sexy, I like you.

When a mother asks her son if he put out the garbage yet and he raises his eyebrows once, it means, Yes or, Maybe.

And if a guy lowers his eyebrows at another guy—*malagu hao mumu?*

Watch out. Fists are about to fly.

New Girl Day

At lunch, I don't hear Tonya's jokes or Delia's new gossip about what Lola did with Carlos when her parents went to visit her sick nana. I'm too busy watching Mary Kelly. She's sitting next to the girls who make straight As, read required books, and wear their socks cuffed. Not like Delia, Tonya, and me. We skid by with Cs, skim Cliffs Notes for assigned books, and roll down our socks until the sisters catch us. Mary Kelly settles next to the Brains, but it's like she's alone, curled over the table, eating her peanut butter and jelly sandwich.

At recess, she sits with her back pressed against the outside wall, watching Olivia and the other little girls dance. Can't she figure out that's the kiddy side of the school yard? The part of the playground with hopscotch squares, swings, and slides? Stupid girl. That's no way to make friends.

An Admirer

"He likes you, girl," Teresita tells me.

"Roman? You're *kaduka*."

Teresita and Roman have most classes together. "All day at school, he asks about you. Do you think Isabel will run for fiesta queen? Do you think Isabel is studying algebra in school? Maybe she can help me. Do you think Isabel will be working at the store today?"

"What do you tell him?"

"I answer, 'Absolutely no.' 'I have no idea.' And, 'Of course.'"

"Just because he asks those questions doesn't mean anything."

She pokes me in the ribs with her elbow. "Yeah, he likes you, Isabel."

I glare at Teresita, but all I can think of is that I don't have room in my life for anyone else.

Suruhana

Auntie Bernadette's back porch is her office. A bed is out there for patients to lie on. Blinds hang over the screens, blocking the bright sun, and a small rotating fan stirs the heat.

Today she watches the clock with one eye while she rubs herbs on the old man's throat and massages it with a spoon.

"Watch, Isabel, watch carefully," she tells me. "One day it will be you standing here." She says this like it's a great honor to be a *suruhana*.

I don't want people knocking on my door day and night, asking for me to heal them. No way.

But Auntie Bernadette tells me, "You're destined for this." Her mother, my grandmother, was a *suruhana,* as was her mother before her. Then she adds, "You were born feetfirst."

Her words sting. She might as well have said I was

born with a huge purple mark on my cheek. At least then no one would expect me to heal them.

Auntie Bernadette talks faster about the night I was born, but my mind blurs and her voice becomes a hum. I concentrate on the sounds of the ocean crashing against the huge rocks outside her screen porch. I try to ignore Auntie's jars of dried herbs along the wall and her chickens prancing in the backyard that she raises just for their feathers, an added ingredient to some special cures.

I stare at the old man with the wrinkled back. His skin is yellow like chicken fat. Surely this isn't my destiny. Auntie rubs the spoon deeper into the back of the man's neck.

"Ay-yi!" The man arches his back, his eyes wide.

"Almost done," Auntie says, pushing him back down.

Again she looks at the clock. Finally I realize it's Wednesday, bingo night. She doesn't want to be late.

Bingo and Cockfights

"Do away with all gambling," Auntie Bernadette often says. "The greyhound races, cockfights, but not bingo." Bingo used to be sponsored by the Catholic Church, and Auntie Bernadette believed it was her duty as a good Catholic to support the church. After so many people lost their grocery and rent money on bingo night, the Catholic Church stopped sponsoring the games. But Auntie Bernadette still goes every Wednesday night.

I'm not allowed to play, but I've gone with her. She knows all the games—double bingo, crazy kite, broken picture frame, and many more. She plays five cards at once and when she wins, she jumps and waves her good hand in the air. "Bingo! Bingo!" she shouts.

A man scrambles over to check her numbers. Once she won a thousand dollars. She bought dresses for Olivia and me and shirts for Frank. Even though it was a lot of money, I'm sure the bingo sponsors have gotten every penny back from her, plus a lot more.

If Auntie Bernadette had her way and the government made cockfights illegal, Teresita wouldn't be the only one to miss them. Even my father grumbles when the animal rights people protest. "Those Humane Society people don't know anything," he says. "They think cockfights are cruel. ESPN shows people shooting ducks. What's the difference? Millions of people watch the duck hunts. Only a few watch cockfights."

Though Tata has never returned to the Dededo dome after someone keyed his truck, he likes to go to cockfights held at fiestas or the sneaky ones at Saturday night barbecues. Big money seldom changes hands there like at the dome, mostly just cases of beer.

Not Now

Olivia dances around the house, wearing my mother's fiesta queen tiara. As she dances, she strums Mom's ukulele, singing a song she made up. The words sort of sound like one Mom sang when she was acting silly, playing "Tiptoe Through the Tulips" on top of the coffee table. But Olivia sings, "Tiptoes and two lips."

Frank laughs, and the sound startles me. He hasn't laughed since before my mother died. But something about Olivia's song and dance bothers me. The skin on my face prickles. I grit my teeth and sit on my hands to keep from grabbing the ukulele. I turn on the television and stare at the screen. She plucks the strings hard and sings louder, prancing in front of the TV, staring my way. I look right through her. She is glass.

Tata enters our house, carrying an ice chest. His lips grip a cigarette, but when he sees Olivia, the cigarette falls to the tiled floor and he drops the ice chest on the table.

"Stop!" He lunges toward her, grabbing the ukulele.

I haven't heard Tata yell since Frank almost drowned. Olivia whimpers and Tata kneels next to her. In the kitchen, a string of cigarette smoke swirls high into the air.

"Not now," Tata says softly, stroking Olivia's hair. "Later."

Frank slinks lower on the couch and stares up at the ceiling. Relieved, I breathe again.

Breakfast of Champions

Tata is usually gone by sunrise, so I'm surprised to see him in the kitchen this morning, opening cabinets and slamming them shut. His jaw tightens as he peers at Frank from the corner of his eye. Frank sits in my mother's seat, eating his cereal. Even though the three of us continue to change chairs at each meal, no one has ever sat in my mother's seat until now.

Frank keeps eating, his chin resting on his fist.

"Where's the rice?" Tata asks me. He's used to eating fried Spam, rice, and Tabasco sauce in the mornings.

"We finished it last night," I say. "And there's no Spam in the house. Do you want me to run over to the store and get some?"

Tata shakes his head and returns the frying pan, then slams the cabinet door. Frank doesn't blink an eye. He doesn't even bat an eyelash when Tata yanks the cereal box from the table, even though Frank was reading the back of the box. Now he stares at the space in front of him.

Two men, few words, their actions loud as warriors.

Tata eats his breakfast in the living room on the couch, holding his bowl right below his chin. "You need to find another place to sit," he says as he leaves the house for the day. There are three of us at the table, but I know he's talking to Frank.

When Frank
Almost Drowned

Frank almost drowned four years ago, when he was seven. Auntie Bernadette used to call Frank "Two Step" because he was always two steps behind Tata, happy to walk in his shadow. One day Frank begged and begged Tata to let him go along on his fishing trip, but Tata told Frank no. He was going out with a couple of friends on their new boat. He probably didn't think it would be right to ask Frank along since it wasn't his boat. Maybe he should have told Frank that. Instead he said, "Go play with your toys," as if he were swatting away a fly.

That morning I saw Frank in the backyard, his head pressed against a coconut tree, kicking the trunk. He kept kicking and kicking until I ordered him to stop. Later in the day, when my father returned home, Frank bragged to some boys that he was going to swim to Cocos Island, a mile away.

I don't know anyone who has swum to Cocos Island.

I don't know anyone who would want to. But Frank was young and I believe he was trying to impress my father. So he thought nothing of making a bet with those older boys, who knew better. Roman was one of those boys.

When Frank was almost out of sight, Roman got scared. I guess he started thinking, What if Frank drowned? What if this silly boy didn't have enough sense to turn around when he tired?

Finally Roman went for my father, who was at the cabana, cleaning fish. My father kicked off his zoris, crossed the street in bare feet, raced to the beach, and took off swimming. With Olivia on my hip, I watched from the shore, helpless.

Frank's foot began to cramp. He wrestled the waves, trying to gasp for air, swallowing enough water to fill a bucket. Tata reached him just in time.

The next thing I knew, Frank was lying on the beach unconscious, and Tata was beating his stomach with tight fists, shouting, "My son, why?"

Auntie Bernadette showed up, half of her hair rolled in hot curlers. She fell to her knees next to Tata. "Move, Vincent!"

Tata slowly stepped away and Auntie Bernadette performed mouth-to-mouth resuscitation. I'd never seen anyone do this before, so it appeared strange to me—my auntie's mouth covering my brother's. With each breath, curls unraveled from her rollers, one by one, until they each lay on the sand.

Water foamed from Frank's mouth, followed by a gush. He coughed and coughed, then started to breathe in great big gasps.

Tata cried and hugged Frank tight. But it's the last time I can remember him doing that. Now Roman walks in my father's shadow. Maybe Tata's ashamed of Frank because since that day, Frank will only go into the ocean when the tide is low on a full-moon night. It's sad. Frank tried to win my father's love by conquering the water. Now it's the water that keeps them apart.

Where Was She?

When I think back to the day that Frank almost drowned, I wonder, Where was my mother?

The Dream

Last night I dreamed about the Fragrant Lady. The legend of the Fragrant Lady goes way back. Auntie Bernadette told me about her when I was five years old. That day the sky was clear and blue, and the sweetest scent drifted in the air.

I asked Auntie Bernadette, "What flower makes that smell?"

"Must be the Fragrant Lady," she told me. "At a certain time of the year a sweet lemony scent floats around the island. But no one on the island can find a flower that makes that scent. Many have tried and failed," she said. "It doesn't grow on Guam.

"Someone decided it must be the Fragrant Lady. She bathes in the ocean with the oil from the flower. Nobody has ever seen her face, but they know she's there because of the sweet, sweet smell.

"Once a curious man searched for her in the mountains above his home. He caught a glimpse of her, a woman wearing a long white dress. But he was not happy with that small peek. He followed her to the ocean. Just as he spotted her in the water, she waved, then vanished. Nobody to this day has seen her face."

Last night, in my dream, I smelled the sweet scent. Like the man, I followed the Fragrant Lady into the mountains, then to the sea. I even went into the ocean and swam closer to her. She waved and disappeared. I never saw her face.

Robbed

If Olivia had a nightmare last night, I didn't hear her because I slept straight through. But this morning I feel hot and exhausted instead of rested. My hair and clothes are soaked from sweat, not from Olivia's big spot of pee on the sheet. My throat hurts when I swallow.

I want to call out for my mother, but when I try to think of her, my mind grows fuzzy. My heart races and my head pounds. I close my eyes and try to recall her face, her smell, her touch. It's no use. I can't remember my mother at all.

Pictures

"You have a fever," Auntie Bernadette tells me as she rubs some herbal potion on my throat. "You'll remember your mother when you're well. Now rest."

When she leaves, I walk through our empty house in search of proof. I see my mother as a young girl, eight or nine years old, eating a mango, her long black hair blowing in the wind. I see her at fifteen, smiling with a crown on her head at the Malesso fiesta. I see her at eighteen in a long white dress, dancing with my father at their wedding.

I try hard to remember my mother at home. Squeezing my eyes shut, I think back to birthdays, Christmases, rosaries, weddings. I know she was there. The pictures prove it.

Chicken Noodle Soup

"Your mother was fiesta queen two years in a row," Auntie Bernadette tells me as she places a bowl of Campbell's chicken noodle soup in front of me. "She loved to play the ukulele and had a laugh that made you want to host a fiesta for no special reason." Auntie Bernadette feeds me memories by the spoonful.

Then she serves me a cup of tea she makes from *amot*. Her medicines come from the jungles and pots of herbs she grows in her backyard.

What must life have been like for Auntie Bernadette to have a beautiful younger sister everyone admired? I never thought about that until today after studying the pictures.

I'm curious if Auntie Bernadette married an old man because he was probably the only one who asked her. Uncle Fernando is older than God, eighty-something years old. When they lit the candles on his last birthday cake, I thought the house would burn down.

"Maybe you can run for fiesta queen," Auntie Bernadette says. "You're pretty enough to win two years in a row, too. I could make your pageant dress like I did for Erlinda."

I don't want to follow the footsteps of someone I don't remember. That would be like chasing a ghost that doesn't want to be caught.

God's Instrument

Uncle Fernando has children from his first wife who are now grandparents. He married Auntie Bernadette after his wife died, but they never had children of their own. I believe Uncle Fernando married Auntie Bernadette because she was a *suruhana*. He always complains about his head aching, his heart racing, or his bowels acting up. We don't want to eat around Uncle Fernando because he tells us how what we're eating is going to make us sick. "That *kelaguen* will give you the runs," or, "If you eat too many betel nuts, you will get drunk in the head."

"Fernando is from Umatac," Auntie Minerva says. "They used to marry their sisters in that village." She states this like it explains everything strange about Uncle Fernando.

Most days Uncle Fernando sits on the couch and watches TV or lies in his bed. From couch to bed, bed to couch. I'm sure he did something else when he was younger, but I don't know what it was.

Auntie Bernadette makes herself available to everyone. "Healing is my gift," she says. "It's my responsibility."

The only time she refuses to help someone is if they are sick with *taotaomo'na* disease. "I can't cure what is meant to be. Besides, they should know better than to disrespect our ancestors."

Most days, people come to her home with sore throats. She massages them with spoons, feeds them herbs, places her hands on their necks. Then they leave. When they awake the next morning, they are healed, but then Auntie Bernadette usually catches their sore throat. The funny thing is when she's sick, she takes Tylenol.

"Why don't you take the herbs?" I asked her once.

"Because I believe the Tylenol works," she said. "And it does. My customers believe my herbs and my touch heal them and it does. Of course our heavenly Father heals them. I am only his instrument."

Playing Hooky

I nap on and off all morning. Auntie Bernadette slips in and out of the house. Later I wake to the sound of a stick being stroked down the typhoon shutters covering my windows. *Rut-t-ton, rut-t-ton.* When I push one slat open to peek, two eyes stare back. I jump and yelp.

Teresita steps back. "Don't go *kaduka,* girl. It's me."

It's one o'clock in the afternoon. "Why aren't you in school?"

"Test day!" she announces. "Don't want to flunk."

Teresita is lying. She's smart and doesn't have to study to make the honor roll.

"What's wrong with you?" she asks.

"I'm sick, but how did you know I was home?"

"I saw your father. He told me." Tata will never tattle on Teresita, but he'll use her skipping school as an example of bad behavior.

"Guess what? My mother might visit today."

Teresita never mentions her mother.

"She broke up with her boyfriend, and she's been going to rehab."

"That's great," I tell her, but something stirs in my stomach.

"Too bad you're sick," she says. "You could watch me box."

Teresita is playing hooky so she can train her chickens. She wants to be the big winner at the fiesta cockfight.

Another Visitor

After Teresita leaves, I drift back to sleep, listening to the radio. This time I awake to Roman's voice calling me outside my window.

"Isabel?"

I open the shutters. "Why aren't you in school?" Today must be the day for playing hooky.

"It's four-thirty. I've been home for half an hour."

I stare at the clock. He's right. Somehow I've slept for three hours. Olivia's book bag is in the corner of the room. How did I miss so much?

"Isabel, I wanted to see how you were. Can I get you anything?"

"No. But maybe if people would quit hanging around my window, I could get well."

"I better go. I told your father that I'd help him repair his net today."

I watch him walk away until I can't see him anymore.

Musical Chairs

Miss one day from school and the world changes. At lunch Mary Kelly sits in my usual spot beside Tonya.

"Excuse me, miss," I tell her, my hand on my hip.

Across the table, Delia scoots over and pats the space next to her. "Sit here, Isabel."

I've sat where Mary Kelly is sitting for the last two years. I think about how we swap chairs at home for every meal and my vow to never have a special seat. But this is different. This is school.

Mary Kelly opens her brown paper sack and passes around Fruit Roll-Ups. I tried them once, when an air force guy gave some to Tata in trade for a gallon of *tuba*. That day Frank, Olivia, and I had bellyaches from eating so many.

Delia takes a grape one. Tonya chooses lime. I shake my head. None for me, thank you.

"Mary Kelly invited us to the base pool Saturday," Delia says.

Mary Kelly smiles at me. "You can come, too."

I stare at her a long moment, then ask, "Why aren't you sitting with the Brains?"

She looks at Delia and Tonya. The three of them smile at one another. "I like to laugh," she says.

Impostor

In choir, Mary Kelly sings the "Guam Hymn" louder than anyone else. When we sing the new song, the one that the sisters let us snap our fingers to, she leans forward and shakes her shoulders.

Mary Kelly winks and smiles at the boys when they raise their eyebrows at her. She makes Lola look like a saint.

She eats green mangoes dipped in hot sauce and salt without squinting. She dances with Olivia and the little kids at recess. She even talks like us now, her words slipping up and down.

"Mary Kelly is one of us," Delia says. Tonya agrees. Not me.

Who does this haole think she is, pretending to be a Chamorro?

No-show

Teresita's mother didn't show up the other day.

"Should've known," Teresita says. "She couldn't remember to feed me when I lived with her. How could she remember to visit?"

"Maybe something came up," I say, but I'm thinking the worst. Maybe she got a hit of ice. I hear that stuff is bad.

"Oh, she called the next day. Her counselor said she wasn't ready yet."

"What does that mean?"

"Who knows? Who cares?" Teresita picks up a rock and throws it toward the jungle. That means end of subject.

Olivia's Crab

Olivia catches a land crab and brings it to me in a bucket. I shake my head, frowning. "You know you're not supposed to catch crabs until we go crabbing on the full-moon night. Tata will be angry."

Olivia ignores me. "I'm going to feed my crab coconut for two days and make him fat before I eat him."

"And who is going to cook one crab?" I ask.

She puts him inside Tata's crab cage in the cabana. For two days she feeds him coconut and for two days I wait to hear Tata say something about it. But he never does.

Wednesday night, Auntie Bernadette comes to our house. She fills our smallest pot with water and puts it on the stove.

A few minutes later, I ask her, "What are you making?"

"Olivia's dinner," she says, then drops the crab into the boiling water.

Don't You Remember?

Auntie makes fried rice in our kitchen while she asks, "Don't you remember when your mother tried to enroll you in ballet class, but you cried so much, she brought you home?"

"No," I say.

Olivia is sitting at the table, trying to open her crab's claw with a nutcracker. "Why didn't she put me in ballet lessons?"

Why didn't she? I wonder.

Auntie stirs the scrambled eggs into the rice. "Do you remember when your mother taught you to swim at the pool by the mayor's office?"

I shake my head.

"Isabel taught me to swim," Olivia says.

"Of course you remember the silly songs she made up?"

"Auntie," I say, "don't forget to add the onions." I want her to stop this quizzing.

"I remember the silly songs," Olivia says, then begins to sing "Hiccups and Hibiscus."

"You better finish your crab," I tell her. "It lost its life to be your dinner."

Auntie scoops some fried rice into a bowl for her and Uncle Fernando, then motions me to follow her to the front door. "I should have talked about your mother more before now. Forgive me. I guess I didn't want to make you sad. But Isabel, you must try to remember. Remember the good, forget the bad."

Ana, Who Likes
Animal Crackers,
Peanut Butter, and Comics

Ana Cruz comes by our store today. I try not to stare at her big round belly, but it's hard to avoid it. Ana has always been skinny. She looks so different now. Like a gingerbread girl who's been rolled out wider with a rolling pin. Auntie Bernadette says she can always tell when a Chamorro girl is pregnant because her nose spreads. Ana is half Chamorro. I study her nose.

Ana strolls down the aisles. She picks up a box of animal crackers and peanut butter and goes over to the shelf where we keep newspapers, magazines, and comic books. She flips through a Superman comic book. It's well-worn.

"They're all old. I forgot to order some new ones." I don't tell her that Tata said that he wasn't going to order any more. Everyone reads them. No one buys. He told me to tell the customers, "If you read, you purchase." But I ignore his advice and let people read them. I even let some of the boys take them to the cabana.

Ana continues to read, then carries it over to the register to buy with her cookies and peanut butter.

"Half price," I tell her when I ring in the comic. "It's so old anyway."

"Thanks," she says, then shyly glances at her stomach. "I guess you know that I'm going to have a baby?"

"Uh, yes. Congratulations."

"Dominic is the father."

"That's what I figured. Since you're always together. I mean since you're going out."

"Your auntie says it's a girl."

I nod. "She should know."

Taotaomo'na

"I don't believe in ghosts!" Mary Kelly takes a bite of pickled papaya and smacks her lips.

Mary Kelly laughs at the *taotaomo'na*. She thinks the *taotaomo'na* is made up like Santa, something you believe in when you're little and grow out of. That girl better watch out. I know firsthand what can happen if someone messes around and doesn't respect the *taotaomo'nas*.

"Where is he?" Mary Kelly asks when I tell her *taotaomo'nas* live in banyan trees like the one we're sitting under.

"*Taotaomo'nas* are not he," I say. "*They* are our ancient ancestors."

"Don't go into the jungle without their permission," Delia says.

Mary Kelly presses her hands together and looks up at the tree. "Please, O mighty *taotaomo'nas*, may I go in the jungle?" She snickers.

"You better be careful," I say. "Once Frank peed in the jungle and he didn't ask permission. He woke up with a terrible sore throat and a big bruise on his arm."

"Maybe he caught strep throat at school," Mary Kelly says. "Maybe he bruised his arm in the jungle."

Delia leans forward. "My father knows the jungle better than anyone. One day he forgot to ask permission to go into the jungle. He said that even though he walked a straight line, he ended up at the same spot where he started from, as if he'd walked in a circle."

"Yeah," I say, "Auntie Bernadette knows three pregnant women whose babies were snatched from their bellies." I clap. "Just like that. Gone!"

The other girls nod.

"That's right," Delia says.

"Be careful," Tonya adds.

Mary Kelly's face turns kind of green. "Stop! I don't want to hear any more." She doesn't say another word the rest of recess.

Finally some respect!

Evening Watch

Tonight I pat Olivia's back and wait for her nightmare to pass, then take a deep breath and shut my eyes. Just as I'm about to fall asleep, I hear a scratching sound coming from the other side of the wall. I ease out of bed, walk into the hall, and peek inside Frank's room.

Frank lies on his side, his back to me. The night-light's glow captures the shadow of his hand moving across the wall. Then I notice the small pocketknife he got for Christmas two years ago. Frank's hand is wrapped around it in a tight fist. He's carving into the wall. I step back from the doorway, walk down the hall, and slip into my bed.

The Marks on Frank's Wall

I hate you.

I hate you.

I hate you.

I hate you.

I hate you.

I hate you.

A Stranger in the House

There is a stranger in our house. He looks like Frank, pretty Frank, his bangs always falling over the long eyelashes girls go crazy over. My brother, who stood in front of the entire church and sang "Ave Maria" last year. His voice was so pure and clear that it made women dig in their purses for tissue. Frank, who knew every knock-knock joke by heart.

Where is that Frank?

At the kitchen table I try to search in his eyes, but he grabs the cereal box, holds it in front of his face, and reads. Where is the boy who couldn't care less about how many fortified vitamins are in Froot Loops?

Not a Rose

Mary Kelly shows off the yellow flower Dan Hernandez gave her. Delia hides her mouth, but I laugh, loud and long. For a moment, it makes me forget about Frank.

Dan gave Mary Kelly a *take'biha*. In English that means old woman's poop!

Is He the One?

After school today, Tata mows the lawn while Frank throws rocks and cut grass into the jungle. I watch them from the cabana. Sometimes they're only a few feet away from each other, but even if they spoke, the lawn mower would prevent them from hearing their words.

Is he the one who Frank hates?

Ana Cruz Gives Birth

The phone rings. It's after ten o'clock, too late for Delia to call. Her mother doesn't believe in calling people past nine.

"Isabel." Auntie Bernadette's voice is breathless and filled with excitement like when she wins at bingo. "Come over to Mrs. Cruz's house now. Ana is about to give birth."

"Why do I have to be there?"

"I might not be around one day and you'll need to know what to do. Besides, don't you want to see a miracle?"

"Auntie, I haven't finished my homework. I'll see the baby tomorrow."

I hang up the phone. I've never used homework as an excuse before, but I don't want Auntie to turn me into a midwife. Still, when I close my eyes tonight, I can't help but think that I'm missing out on something.

Watch Me

"Your sister needs you," Sister Agnes tells me in the middle of science class.

Olivia is at the door with one of her friends. Her damp bangs stick to her forehead, the way they do when she's been playing outside all day. Her white uniform shirttail hangs over her skirt.

"Will you come watch me dance?" she asks.

"Olivia," I whisper, "I'm in the middle of science."

"At lunch, then, please?" She has second recess during my lunch period.

"Okay, I'll see you at lunch. Now go."

She and her friend skip away, holding hands.

When I return to my desk, I flip to the back of my notebook, where I wrote today's list. I add to the bottom: Remind Olivia to keep her blouse tucked in.

Watching Olivia Dance
Outside the Cafeteria

Olivia dances like she has no troubles—
shakes her body, head to toe,
taps her feet to the beat of the drum.
She is the guitar's vibration,
the soprano's highest note.
When the music slows, she moves
like a coconut palm, swaying
in an island breeze.
She thinks she's onstage in front of an adoring audience.
Never mind that the music plays from
Carlos's radio propped in the cafeteria window and
that almost everyone in the crowd
is just now learning how to multiply.

Closed Doors

*O*ur home has turned into a house with closed doors. My morning begins when I hear Tata shutting the front door as he leaves to fish. Olivia used to leave the bathroom door open, even when she was on the toilet. "Shut the door," I'd tell her. "No one wants to smell your stink." Now she locks the door and spends so much time in there, I worry that her little heinie has fallen through the commode.

Today after school Frank slips into his room and closes the door behind him like a thief hiding out. I bang on his locked door. "What are you doing in there?"

"Homework."

What goes on in his room besides homework? I wish he was like Olivia, letting the cha-cha do its magic.

How can any spirits move around our house with so many closed doors? Maybe they wait until night, when we leave doors open so that the air from the air conditioner in the front window can circulate through our house.

Does my mother's spirit still live here?

A Different Hat

Sister Rachel brings three boxes of costumes to English class today. "We're going to role-play our favorite characters from literature," she tells us. "A game of charades, except you'll say something that your character might say. Then everyone will try to guess the identity."

The students groan but rush to the boxes like they're checking out their Christmas stockings. Sister Rachel brought lots of hats, a few capes, and even some fake mustaches and beards. I try to find an item that reminds me of something Jane Eyre would wear and settle for a lacy white bow attached to a hair clip.

I run the story through my mind like a movie. Even though I've read the book five times, I can't decide on a scene I'd want to share with the class. They're all too special and personal, as if sharing would be like telling a friend's secret. Because somehow when I read that book, I feel like I'm the only one who knows Jane's life.

At my desk, I ponder some of the best scenes, while across the room Sister Rachel stands behind some of the girls admiring themselves in a mirror. She's wearing a lady's hat from the forties and her uni-brow is completely covered by the brim. To my surprise, she tilts her head to the right and stares at her image a long moment, then glances quickly around as if to see if anyone noticed her studying her reflection. And for some reason, my heart aches.

It's a Girl

On the way home from school, Auntie told us that Ana Cruz gave birth to a girl late this morning. She had a long, hard delivery. That's why Auntie didn't make our dinner this afternoon. She was home, taking a nap.

John Wayne wanted his sister to name the baby Miss Kitty, after the redheaded lady who owns the saloon on the *Gunsmoke* reruns. Ana named the baby Carmella.

I wonder if Carmella will like to dance. And I wonder if one day it will bother her that her father isn't married to her mother.

Parents Night

Mary Kelly's mother is expecting a baby. Mary Kelly never told us, but tonight is Parents Night at school, and I see Mrs. Johnson's stomach poking out like a pumpkin. Maybe that's why Mary Kelly hated the stories about babies being snatched from their mothers' bellies.

Tonight Mary Kelly turns back into the new girl on the first day. She acts shy, barely saying hi to me. But when her mother touches her arm, Mary Kelly pulls back like she's embarrassed of her.

Auntie Bernadette is here instead of Tata because someone had to go to Frank's school. During the cookie reception, she walks across the room to Mrs. Johnson. And like she does to every pregnant woman she sees, Auntie places her good hand on Mrs. Johnson's big belly, closes her eyes, and makes her prediction. "Boy!" she announces confidently.

Mrs. Johnson's eyes pop wide. "I beg your pardon?" she asks in a Scarlett O'Hara accent.

"You're going to have a boy. No question." Auntie Bernadette smiles, pleased with herself.

"Well, actually I had the amniocentesis and the test results say it's a girl."

"No, the test is wrong. The baby is a boy."

Mrs. Johnson rubs her lower back.

"I'll get you some of my special tea. It will help with your backaches and later with labor."

My face feels hot. Mary Kelly's father is a doctor. They don't believe in Chamorro potions and cures.

Mrs. Johnson smiles in a way that makes me think she doesn't believe Auntie Bernadette. She smiles like she will get in the car with Mary Kelly later tonight and they'll laugh at what Auntie Bernadette said.

Mary Kelly leans over toward my ear and whispers, "Want a cigarette?"

We sneak out of the room, slip into a bathroom stall, and smoke our troubles away.

Full Moon

Friday is a full-moon night, the best time to go crabbing. Around the island people head for the rivers and the beaches. With flashlights in hand, we go—Olivia, Frank, Tata, Auntie Bernadette, Roman, and me. The night air is warm and thick with mosquitoes, so we dress in long sleeves and pants.

Usually Roman is near Tata, but tonight he stays by me, showing off. He's practiced Tata's technique to perfection, even catching the crabs bare-handed. The rest of us wear rubber gloves. Roman steps on a crab, grabs it from behind so it won't pinch him with its claws, pulls it out of the water, and throws it into the bucket.

"See, Isabel, you must be quick," Roman says.

I don't like to crab, but I like being out in the water at dark. Tonight the perfect round moon casts its white glow down on the ocean and the flashlights dance like tiny diamonds on the black water.

There are groups of two or more scattered about with buckets and sacks. Closer to the shore, Frank stands alone. I feel like I should go to him. But he'd move away and make his own space again.

Roman lifts another crab. "See, Isabel, see."

"I need to help Olivia," I tell him.

As I walk away, he calls out, "What happened to you?"

I turn. "What do you mean?"

"You used to be fun. Now you're so serious . . . like an old lady."

I shoot a look at him that could kill every crab in the ocean. And I walk away thinking how I have forgotten not only my mother but also the girl Roman says that I used to be.

Legend of
Santa Marian Kamalen

The people of Malesso may eat crabs, but there are two special crabs we pay homage to. They're next to Santa Marian Kamalen on Malesso's flag.

One day, Olivia asked me about those crabs.

"They're a reminder of a miracle," I told her. "Over three hundred years ago a statue of Santa Marian Kamalen floated to our shores escorted by two crabs with lighted candles on their backs."

"How could they hold the candles?" Olivia asked.

"Olivia, let me finish the story. A fisherman saw the miracle, but when he got closer, the statue drifted away from him. When he fully clothed himself, he was able to reach her. He presented the statue of Our Lady to the Spanish governor. And you know what?"

"What?" asked Olivia.

"The crabs with candles are only a part of the miracle.

The statue is made of ironwood. Ironwood doesn't float."

"Then how can it float?"

I sighed. Some people don't know how to just accept a miracle.

Nightly Ritual

At eleven I check to see if Tata has switched from the floor to his bed. He hasn't. I cover him with a blanket as I've done almost every night since we returned a month ago. The beer must help him sleep soundly because he doesn't even stir.

Back in my room, I stare at the ceiling, trying to remember how to make the *golai hagun sune*. I can only recall the coconut. Olivia's nightmare comes and goes, we visit the bathroom, and then I fall asleep to the sound of scratches.

Gone

Teresita spits on the ground. "My uncle sold my chickens," she says. "He tricked me. He asked me which of the chickens were the best fighters. I told him. Then he sold them."

"Why did he sell them?" I ask her.

Teresita is boiling in her own stew and doesn't hear me. Back and forth she paces. "All year long, I've trained my chickens. I picked the best ones and spent at least an hour a day boxing them."

"Teresita, why did he sell them?"

She takes a big breath. "He said he needed the money. He's probably right. He makes so many bad bets. My uncle has even bet against his own chickens and lost. Such an idiot! But selling them isn't the worst part." She swallows and takes a deep breath. "Isabel, he sold them to Lorenzo."

She boxes the air. *Bam, bam, bam.* And I'm certain if Lorenzo or her uncle had been standing there, they'd be flat on the ground.

The Christening of Carmella Iglesias Martina Cruz Flores

Today the priest christens Ana's baby. Her full name is Carmella Iglesias Martina Cruz Flores. Her father, Dominic, keeps his arm around Ana. He won't quit grinning either. He acts like he did something special. Like he lay in bed, for nine hours, with his knees against his chest and squeezed out a baby. All he did was unzip his pants, then, probably five minutes later, zip them back up.

Dominic's brother is the godfather and Auntie Bernadette is the godmother. She must be the godmother to a hundred children. What is she going to do if one day someone gives her all those kids? Feed them herbs? She collects babies like Auntie Minerva collects religious plates. I hope she never has to make room for them.

Auntie Bernadette's
Baby Fiesta

Every year Auntie Bernadette hosts a fiesta for the babies that she delivered into the world. She also invites the babies that were conceived after she treated their mothers, and her godchildren. Some of those babies are now my age. Some are grown-ups with babies of their own.

A newspaper photographer takes a picture of Auntie and all her "children." The next morning, Frank and I can't wait to open the paper and count the crying babies. The record was two years ago—twenty-seven squalling babies. Auntie was in the center, smiling like the proud godmother.

A Proposal

Mrs. Cruz hosts the reception following Carmella's christening. Her backyard reminds me of a regular fiesta, with three tables put together to make one long table for the food. After everyone's bellies are filled with red rice, grilled eggplant, tamales, and fish, Dominic lifts his beer can high in the air. "Excuse me, everyone," he yells over and over until only the Chamorro music playing from a CD player can be heard.

Even Ana stares up at him from her lawn chair like she wishes he'd sit. Carmella's chin rests on her shoulder as Ana pats her back. Dominic kneels in front of Ana and some of the women say, "Ohhh!"

Doesn't he know the man is supposed to kneel on one knee?

Dominic pulls a gold ring with a tiny diamond from his back pocket and grabs Ana's left hand away from Carmella. Sweat beads run down his face and his shirt has two wet spots underneath the armpits.

"Ana, will you marry me?"

Ana looks down, embarrassed, and pulls her hand away and starts to pat Carmella's back. For a moment I think she's going to say no. I even feel sorry for Dominic, kneeling there, waiting. But then Carmella burps loud and everyone laughs. Ana smiles and nods at Dominic, who seems relieved. He tries to slip the ring on her finger, but it won't fit. Finally the ring makes a nice pinky ring. The women rush up to Ana and the men slap Dominic on the back. Sounds of beer cans snapping open fill the air. A few swigs to celebrate the good news.

I overhear Auntie Bernadette talking to Mrs. Camacho.

"Looks like Lucia Cruz has a wedding to plan," says Auntie.

Mrs. Camacho shakes her head. "First a baby, then a marriage. So many things out of order these days."

Happily Ever After

Teresita shakes her head when Dominic proposes. "It will never last."

"Why not?" I ask.

"If it does last, she'll end up black-and-blue like his mother. Those men in Dominic's family have nasty tempers."

Across the yard, Dominic's mom, Maria Flores, cries and picks up baby Carmella.

"See Mrs. Flores," Teresita says. "She's crying because she knows Ana's destiny. It's the same as hers."

"I think she's crying because she's happy. And Dominic is different than his dad." I want Ana to have a fairy-tale love story like the ones I read about in my romance novels.

Collecting in the Jungle

Auntie Bernadette recruits me to help her hunt for the medicinal herbs she uses in her *amot tininu* and *amot patgon*. We go into the jungle with machetes and buckets. The machetes cut the thick vines that block our way. I pray to the Virgin Mary that we don't see brown tree snakes, not that they would bother us anyway.

Once Auntie Minerva was cooking a stew. She went to the stove to stir it and a brown tree snake peered up at her from the pot with a little potato in its mouth. She quickly covered the stew with the lid, then fainted. Tata said the snake must have crawled through the open window. He teased Auntie Minerva about making brown tree snake stew, but none of us ate it, of course. Ever since then, I don't like stew or going into the jungle or windows left open.

Today the mosquitoes are the only pests. I wish I'd worn long sleeves like Auntie recommended. I'll bite my tongue before I'll let her see me smack the mosquitoes away. We are searching for *kahlao, gaogao,* and *kamachili* and other herbs. We're lucky because Malesso is in the southern part of the island, where the best plants grow. I understand how herbs might cure sickness. That's not so different than medicine, but the other ingredients I'm not so sure about. How can a chicken feather and the urine of the patient's oldest son make any difference? What if the patient doesn't have a son? How could I be a *suruhana* when I question its ways?

Auntie Bernadette is explaining everything she does. She lifts a fern leaf. "See, this is how the *Galak fedda* should look before you take it." She points out another one. Her face scrunches. "Now this one. This one's not so good."

How can I be a *suruhana* when I don't see the difference?

Latte Stones

Deep in the jungle, Auntie and I pass four *latte* stones. They are seen around the island, giant pillars made from stone and coral that once held houses made of grass and palms. They are hundreds of years old, and when we pass them we pay respect. "Rest in peace, dear ancestors," Auntie says. "We don't wish to disturb you. We're only passing by."

I'm glad Auntie says the words so I don't have to.

Mind Your Own Business

Most of the cans of soup are one month from their expiration date, so I move them up front, mark them down, and hang a sign above them—SOUP FOR A STEAL.

I'm dusting the cans when Roman walks in. "What's with Frank?"

I stop, then go back to dusting. "What do you mean?"

"I just passed him on the road. When I said, 'Hey, Frank,' he didn't say anything."

"Maybe he didn't hear you."

"I passed right by him. Did I do something wrong?"

"I don't know. Did you?"

Remember when you almost let Frank drown? Then you became the hero in Tata's eyes? I want to say this, but instead I ask, "How about some tomato soup?"

Shopping Day

Auntie Bernadette drives me to Tamun to meet Tonya and Delia and shop. She lets me out in front of Liberty House department store, where they're supposed to be waiting for me. Mary Kelly is there instead. I didn't know she was invited.

"I'll pick you up two hours from now in this same spot," Auntie Bernadette says, then rushes to Kmart. Auntie Bernadette dreams of being locked up all night inside Kmart. She gets the biggest thrill reading Noxzema jars and comparing toothpaste costs per ounce.

"*Hafa*," Mary Kelly says.

"Hey," I reply, watching down the street for Delia's mother's pickup. One shared cigarette doesn't make us friends.

We wait and wait on the hot concrete. "I'm calling Delia," I say. I walk away to find a pay phone, expecting Mary Kelly to follow, but she stays behind.

Delia answers the phone.

"Where are you, girl?" I ask.

"My mother's pickup needs a new battery."

"Why didn't you tell me?"

"It just happened," she says. "How was I supposed to know?"

"Well, is Tonya going to pick you up?"

"She was going to ride with me. Her mom left earlier in their car, so I guess we won't be there."

"Great!" I say, and hang up.

I could walk away and leave Mary Kelly alone in front of Liberty House. I think about doing that a good long while but change my mind. Maybe she has another cigarette tucked in her sock.

Elvis Lives at the
Hard Rock Cafe

"Where is everyone?" Mary Kelly asks.

"Car trouble," I say, wishing I was with Auntie Bernadette, racing down the aisles chasing after Blue Light Specials.

Mary Kelly and I decide we might as well shop. We weave in and out of the boutiques. Japanese tourists with fat wallets are everywhere, walking from the fancy hotels into the stores. Someone has to buy the expensive clothes and goods the stores carry. It isn't us and the salespeople know it. They ignore this Chamorro and haole. Their X-ray eyes see right through to our empty pockets.

After admiring all the things we can't afford, we head over to the Hard Rock Cafe and order a hamburger and fries to share. While we wait, a guy with banana sideburns and sunglasses walks in.

Mary Kelly leans over the table and whispers, "Elvis lives."

I try to frown, but the man does look like Elvis, so I smile and add, "Elvis lives on Guam and traded his pink Cadillac for a water buffalo."

Mary Kelly laughs. We take turns naming the famous customers around us. A woman with hair twisted in a tight bun sits in the corner, writing in a notebook.

"Charlotte Brontë," I say.

Then we both agree *Jane Eyre* is the best book ever written. We talk about how we're in love with Mr. Rochester and how we think Jane should have lived in sin with him after she discovered he was married to the loony in the attic.

Our meal arrives. We dab greasy french fries in a pool of ketchup and watch tourists with shopping bags walk along the street. Red trolley cars pass by with more Japanese shoppers.

"Tamun reminds me of Tokyo," Mary Kelly says. "My parents and I spent a few days in Japan on the way over here. We're going to Disneyland when we move back to the States. Have you ever been?"

I shake my head.

"We visited when I was little. We went to the breakfast where the costume characters go and I ate pancakes in the shape of Mickey Mouse. Baby stuff. But there are a lot of cool things to do, too."

I wonder, What's it like to fly in an airplane and get

served ice cream and watch movies above the clouds, like Delia said they do? My feet have never left Guam (except for Cocos Island). What would it be like to be Mary Kelly, flying off every couple of years to other lands?

"Hey," Mary Kelly says, "there's Michael Jackson."

I smile and wonder if the girl sharing french fries with Mary Kelly today would remind Roman of the girl he spoke about on the full-moon night.

Fiesta Queen

"You would make a beautiful fiesta queen," Auntie Bernadette declares, *again,* after mass on Saturday.

I shake my head. "Olivia wants to be fiesta queen. Not me."

"Olivia's day will come. Right now is your turn."

I don't want to wear a tiara and banner and smile at everyone as though winning a pageant were the happiest moment of my life.

"I could make a dress, a red dress or maybe blue like your mother wore." Auntie Bernadette looks up at the ceiling and I know she's already stitching the dress in her mind.

I stare at her like she's *kaduka.* "Auntie, I don't want to be queen of the fiesta."

She doesn't hear me. Her eyes gaze the length of my body, sizing up my waist and hips.

"We're running out of time," she says. "Sophia's

granddaughter has been taking ticket orders for weeks. Although that's illegal."

"Illegal? You mean there are fiesta queen pageant laws?"

"You know what I mean. Tricky, sneaky. Yes, that's it, sneaky. Anyway, you register your name and I'll sell tickets at the bingo games. I'll sell a ton there." She sighs. "Isabel, the dress should be blue. It would be a lucky sign since your mother won twice in blue."

My head pounds. "Auntie!"

"What?"

"I'm not running for fiesta queen, I'm not going to be a *suruhana,* and I'm not making the *golai hagun sune!*"

Auntie Bernadette seems hurt. "Isabel, you don't have to yell."

"I do. You don't listen. I have to yell so you'll hear me."

Auntie Bernadette stares at a Japanese soap opera on TV. Even though Uncle Fernando doesn't understand Japanese, he's usually glued to the soaps, watching the pretty girls. But right now he's asleep, snoring on the couch.

"Isabel," Auntie says, "I haven't mentioned the *golai hagun sune* for weeks."

I don't say anything for a while. She's right. It's me who keeps thinking about it, thinking if I could just remember the recipe, maybe I could remember my mother's face.

After taking a deep breath, I say, "I'm sorry, Auntie Bernadette, but I don't want to be in the pageant." I rush home to the cabana and wait for my father to return with his catch. There are many things I may never do, but one thing is for sure, I'll always clean fish.

A Bridge of Words

Tonight I'm almost asleep when the scratching sounds stop. My heart races. I get out of bed and walk to Frank's doorway. His elbow bent, his head rests on one hand, the knife in the other. He seems to be studying his work, which now includes a bridge of letters the length of his bed.

He lies back flat on his mattress and looks my way. For a moment we stay like that, our eyes locked, but saying nothing. Then he turns toward the wall and begins to scrape again.

The Blue Fabric

Auntie Bernadette calls me to her house. "I have something for you to see," she says. The phone clicks before I
can ask what it is she wants to show me.

Auntie Bernadette's front door is open and I can tell
from the unfamiliar black car parked in her driveway
that a customer must be in the back with her. In the
background, I hear the soft music she plays to relax her
customers.

Uncle Fernando is sleeping on the couch in the living room. The room smells like him—sour milk and the
green onions he chews on. I ease into the chair next to
him and stare at the cartoons. I tap my foot to the clock's
ticking. I turn off the TV with the remote. Uncle Fernando stirs, so I flick *Scooby-Doo* back on. I don't want
to listen to him whine about his aches and pains.

Why did Auntie call for me when she had a customer? Does she want to teach me more of the healing

ways? She makes my blood boil, even though I know all I'd be doing is sitting in the cabana.

I get up and walk around the house. From her bedroom doorway, I discover blue satin fabric spread out on the bed. A closer view reveals a pattern for a long evening dress.

I don't wait any longer. I head home, thinking, What gives my auntie the right to decide who I'm going to be?

Model Mother

When I return home, I find Mrs. Cruz peeking through our store window. John Wayne is squatting under the cabana picnic table, aiming his toy guns my way.

"Bang! Bang!" he says, but I ignore him and look around for Frank, who is nowhere to be found. He was supposed to be watching the store. I want to strangle him, then I remember his wall.

Mrs. Cruz wipes her sweaty forehead with her hand. "I came to buy some chocolate candy for John Wayne."

"Sorry," I tell her. "Frank was supposed to be here."

I open the store and she follows. John Wayne rushes up. "I shot you dead, Isabel."

"John Wayne," Mrs. Cruz says.

"You're supposed to fall down and be dead," he tells me.

"John Wayne," Mrs. Cruz repeats firmly. "Hush and choose some candy."

John Wayne picks up a Milky Way, smells it, then puts

it down and picks up a Snickers. He sniffs a Reese's peanut butter cup, a Mounds, then a pack of plain M&M's.

Hurry, hurry. I need to find Frank. Finally John Wayne selects a Hershey's chocolate almond bar.

"Isabel," Mrs. Cruz says, "when you have a chance, I have something to give you."

I smile and nod, but my gaze is fixed outside the window, searching for my brother. Roman walks toward the store.

Mrs. Cruz shifts her weight from one puffy foot to the other. "I painted a portrait of your mother before . . . before she passed."

My face feels hot. "Oh" is all I can think of to say. The only people I've seen that Mrs. Cruz paints aren't wearing any clothes. I want to remember my mother's face, not learn every mole on her body.

"I think you'd like it," she says.

John Wayne spits out the almonds from his chocolate bar. "Yuck! I hate nuts!"

Roman walks into the store and John Wayne drops the candy bar, draws his pistols, then aims at Roman. "Bang! Bang!"

Without hesitating, Roman slaps his hand over his heart and falls to the floor.

Searching for Frank

At the school yard, Frank's friends look at me with blank stares. "We don't know where he is," they say. "Frank doesn't hang with us anymore. He hasn't for a long time."

"Since we moved back to Malesso?"

"Before that."

"Then who are his friends?" I hope he doesn't hang with the rough gang I heard about.

The boys look at each other, then at me. "Frank wants to be alone now. We try to get him to do stuff with us, but he won't."

I walk toward the pier, thinking how I should have known. We've been back home for over a month. Why didn't I ask Frank why his friends haven't been at the cabana playing *kong-gi* or marbles like they used to? Doesn't Tata notice? Can't he see the words stretching across Frank's wall? Probably not. These days, Tata lives on the sea. He sleeps and eats at our house.

Soon I spot Frank at the park, sitting in front of the statue of Mary, staring out at the ocean. He's wearing a tank top that exposes a fresh scar stretching from his right shoulder down to his elbow. I want to beg him to talk to me, tell me why he doesn't play with his friends or sing his songs, why he tattoos hate into his wall. I want to ask him about the scar.

"Come home, Frank," I tell him. Come back to us.

Inventory

3 butcher
7 butter
5 steak
2 carving
1 paring

Sharp and dull,
I'll count them all
before bed each night.

Roman's Tickets

Roman shows me the five raffle tickets he's bought from one of the candidates of the Malesso Fiesta San Dimas Queen Pageant. Auntie Bernadette was right. Some of these girls start early. This isn't the Miss America Pageant. They know whoever sells the most tickets wins. That's why it doesn't matter what color dress a girl wears or if she's cross-eyed or has a big wart on her nose.

"Five chances," Roman says, waving his tickets. "Five chances for five thousand dollars."

"Or maybe nothing," I say.

"Maybe second place. One thousand dollars." He grins.

"Maybe nothing."

"Or perhaps the refrigerator or freezer."

"Or maybe fifth place," I say. "Three hundred cans of tuna."

"No, I'm going to win big this year. I can feel it."

"That's what Teresita's uncle says every cockfight and look what happened to him. Lost all his chickens."

"This year is different."

"How?" I ask him.

"Well, for one thing, who in a million years thought Teresita would run for queen?"

I give him a look like he's *kaduku*—the craziest boy in Malesso.

"Teresita would never run." I remember last year, when she made fun of the contestants. Teresita twisted her heinie and waved, flashing every tooth in her mouth. We laughed and laughed. I laughed so hard, my side ached.

Teresita, who would rather box chickens than go to Pirate Joe's for a hamburger? Teresita, who never wears a dress, who spits when she's mad, who cusses better than any guy? Not possible.

"Yep, this is my lucky year!" Roman says.

I leave him shuffling his tickets like a gambler with his lucky cards.

The Blue Dress

Auntie Bernadette is making the blue dress for Teresita. She tells me this after she asks why I didn't come by. I tell her I couldn't find Frank to watch the store. I don't want her to know I thought the fabric was for me. I consider telling Auntie about Frank, about the scar, about the words on his wall. But she's too happy, too busy with the dress.

"You're wasting your time making the dress," I say. "Teresita will never go through with it."

"Why do you say that?" she asks.

"Teresita? Cockfighting Teresita?"

"Maybe she knows when to put childish things away and become a young lady."

I sigh. "What did you want, Auntie?"

"I need you to go through your mother's drawers and get her pageant dress." Auntie could do that. There must be some other reason she wants me to sift through my mother's things.

"I made that dress for her."

"Yes." I've heard her say this all my life. How could I not remember? "I don't know what drawer the dress is in."

"Open one drawer. If it isn't there, open another."

"Can't you find it?"

"You're her daughter. I'm her sister. If I hunt for it, people will think I'm a busybody."

"Who would ever think anything like that?"

I say this as if that's exactly what I think, but Auntie Bernadette just strokes the blue satin as if it were a kitten.

The Boy Who Likes to Bleed
by Isabel Moreno

Some can cry
He can only bleed
Every drop of blood
is a tear shed
He wears his scars like badges
for his eyes alone
I wish he'd scream
I wish he'd cry
But he just bleeds

My Essay

The school bell rang five minutes ago and I'm sitting in front of Sister Rachel's desk, staring down at a big fat F on my paper, "The Boy Who Likes to Bleed."

"Who is this boy?" Sister Rachel asks. "This isn't true, is it?"

I study my shoes and shake my head.

"This is more like a poem. The assignment was to write an essay. An essay is based on a true personal experience. Why would you make up such a terrible story when there are so many lovely things that have surely happened to you?"

I shrug and watch a trail of black ants walk across the floor.

"I tell you what, Isabel. I'll give you another chance. Write an essay and this time choose something more pleasant."

She makes me write it before I leave for home. Auntie

Bernadette waits with Olivia in the hallway. Every now and then, Olivia peeks through the window on my classroom door. She sticks out her tongue, she crosses her eyes, she sucks in her cheeks to make fish lips. It doesn't work. I don't laugh. I write.

My Family's Trip to Disneyland

by Isabel Moreno

It's difficult to say what part I enjoyed the most, the ride on the airplane to Los Angeles or Disneyland. On the plane, I watched two movies. I washed my hands with hot wet rags that the flight attendant handed to me with tongs. The trip was so long, I ate two meals and ice cream.

One morning at Disneyland, we had breakfast with Mickey and Minnie Mouse, Donald Duck, and Goofy. The pancakes were shaped like Mickey's face. My mother pulled out her ukulele from its case and Donald Duck begged her to play while my father did the cha-cha with Minnie. Everyone clapped and clapped for my talented parents. They were the stars of the show. I will remember our trip to Disneyland for the rest of my life.

Sister Rachel reads my new essay and smiles. She even laughs, probably at the thought of Tata dancing with Minnie. That *would* have been funny.

Sister Rachel takes her red pen and marks on the top of the page. At home that night I wad up the paper and throw away the only A+ I've received in four years.

Bet

All week I wait for Teresita to come by the cabana and tell me her news. She never does. I have thought of every possible reason that Teresita would run for queen. I even wonder if she's competing so her mother will be proud of her. I know she tries to act tough, like she doesn't care about her mother, but I don't believe her.

When my father returns from fishing on Friday, I take off for Teresita's house. The empty chicken pens in her yard remind me of her uncle's foolish sale to Lorenzo. Her uncle may have paid for the chickens, but they belonged heart and soul to Teresita. She fed them, trained them, sewed them up after wins, buried them after losses.

Teresita sits in front of the TV, playing a video game with her younger cousin, Joel. She looks up and frowns, then tells Joel, "Scram." His eyes stay fixed on the television screen, his fingers punching the buttons on the controller.

Teresita sighs and motions me outside. "Come on."

In her backyard, I ask, "Are you mad at me?"

"Don't be *kaduka*."

"You're the one who's *kaduka*."

Teresita peers toward the jungle.

"Queen?" I say. "Why do you want to be fiesta queen?"

Teresita doesn't say anything.

"You're the one who made fun of those girls, the entire royal court!"

"I don't want to be stupid queen," she says. "I want my chickens back."

"What do chickens have to do with running for queen?"

"Lorenzo told me if I ran for queen and won, he'd give back my chickens."

"What if you lose?"

She stares at the ground. "I have to stay away from any cockfights that he attends."

"Teresita, Lorenzo goes to every cockfight—Dededo, Malesso, all of them."

The way she looks at me, I realize that she already knows this. Teresita has made a pact with the devil.

An Unwelcome Visitor

Frank isn't the only one who bleeds. Today I started my period. I want to tell someone, but who?

For a year I've lied to my friends and told them that I started. Last year Delia went on and on about how Tonya had just got her period. "I started last year," she'd said then. "How about you?"

"Same," I said. How could I tell her any different? She acted like it was a crime to start later than sixth grade.

I didn't know that one lie would turn into many others. Like when Delia and Tonya argued what was best—tampons or napkins—or when they discussed whether or not they should use a vinegar douche the day after their periods ended. I should have stayed quiet, but I thought, Then they'll know. So I said, "Douche, of course." I'd seen the commercials with the ladies in the chiffon nightgowns walking on the beach. They recommended it—feminine freshness, they said. Even though I had no idea what they were talking about.

I have no tampons, sanitary napkins, or vinegar douche. Where's my mother when I need her most?

Auntie Bernadette
to the Rescue

"You are a woman now," Auntie says. This is exactly why I didn't want to ask her for help. But since our store doesn't carry any feminine products, I had no choice.

"We'll drive to the grocery store in Yona. I have to pick up a few items there anyway."

At the store, I select a blue box of tampons, but Auntie shakes her head and selects a huge box of sanitary napkins with wings. "These are best."

I return the tampons to the shelf, now realizing I could have walked to the pier store. They probably had the products there.

When we go to the checkout counter, Auntie tells the cashier, "These aren't for me. That time has passed by. They're for my niece. She's a woman now."

This Week's List for Vendors

7 dozen eggs
7 gallons of milk
2 cases of Coca-Cola
9 cases of Miller Lite
4 cases of Budweiser
3 packages of tampons
2 packages of sanitary napkins

Fittings

Teresita gripes when Auntie Bernadette calls her over for another fitting. She gripes to *me*, not Auntie Bernadette.

"I have to stand on a chair while she pins and makes me turn slowly, then if a customer comes by, she makes me wait. Or if your uncle Fernando needs her to get him a cup of coffee, she stops pinning. Always something."

You should have thought of that before, I want to tell her, but of course, I don't. I'm just glad it's her instead of me. I wouldn't want to parade in front of all of Malesso in a fancy blue dress, no matter how beautiful it is.

I've sold forty tickets for Teresita so far. And no telling how many Auntie Bernadette sold at bingo. Plus she sells to the customers who come for treatments. They buy, hoping their good deed will make them heal quicker. Even Mrs. Camacho bought two tickets when she had Auntie work on her back. And Mrs. Camacho's chubby granddaughter, Margarita, is running for queen.

Ticket Sellers

Auntie Bernadette shakes her head. "You could have been queen the way you sell those tickets."

"I'm selling tickets for Teresita."

Auntie Bernadette takes a stack of ticket booklets with her to bingo and I know she'll come back empty-handed. Those people at bingo will bet on anything, even if it means they might end up with three hundred cans of tuna.

Roman buys four more tickets from me. "You should have ran," he says. "You would have won. *If* you could remember how to smile." He winks.

Maybe if Roman didn't bug me about smiling so much, I would smile. And maybe if Roman didn't hang around Tata so much, my father would see Frank with clear eyes.

Scars

Last night we ate snow cones in the cabana. Olivia accidentally broke the head off her spoon, then dropped it on the ground before running off to play. Frank picked up the spoon. He studied the broken plastic, running his finger over the sharp ridges. Over and over, he rubbed the edges until he caught me staring at him. He squinted at me, then tossed the spoon in the garbage along with his half-eaten snow cone.

I don't know if there's a God anymore, but tonight I pray for more words on Frank's walls. More words, no more cuts.

Bikini Blues

"I hate my mom!" Mary Kelly tells us at recess.

"Why?" Tonya asks.

"She's crazy!"

"*Kaduka?*" Delia asks, then steals a quick glance at me like there's a picture of my mother next to the word in the dictionary.

"Yeah, *kaduka,*" Mary Kelly says. "She won't let me wear a bikini. No two-piece swimsuits. And Mike wants me to wear a bikini."

Mike is Mary Kelly's boyfriend. He's in the navy and she carries a picture of him in her wallet and wears his senior class ring on a chain hidden under her white shirt.

"Would you like to stay over at my house on Friday?" she asks.

"Yeah," we say.

We want a closer look at her *kaduka* mom and sailor boy.

Green-eyed Monster

"Mary Kelly sounds spoiled," Teresita says when I explain why I can't go to the movies with her Friday night. I'll be at Mary Kelly's house on the base. I tell Teresita about how her mother won't allow her to wear a bikini and about her boyfriend, Mike.

"So what?" Teresita scowls. "She can't show off her belly button. And what kind of grown man has a thirteen-year-old girlfriend? She's probably making it up."

That thought crosses my mind, too. I'll find out when we go to the base pool. But somehow I don't think that's why Teresita doesn't like Mary Kelly. She hasn't even met her.

I think about asking Teresita to keep an eye on Frank tomorrow, but then she'd ask why. Instead I say, "Maybe Frank could go with you to the movies."

She says, "Humph!"

"I sold ten more tickets for you."

Teresita raises her eyebrow and says, "That girl is a spoiled haole!"

Second Thoughts

I'm packed to go to Mary Kelly's, but I'm thinking of changing my mind.

Who will see Olivia through her nightmare? Who will cover my father with a blanket if the night turns cool?

Who will make sure Frank only carves his wall?

"Can't I go?" asks Olivia.

For a quick moment, I think about saying yes.

List for Olivia

1. Do your homework
2. Change your clothes before going outside
3. Pick up your nightgown
4. Before bed, brush your teeth and go to the bathroom

A Different Island

Auntie Bernadette drives me to Mary Kelly's house on the base. At the entrance a gate guard stops us and checks for our names on a list, then tells us to come on through. The cream houses lining the street all appear the same, not like Malesso's blue, yellow, and pink ones.

Mary Kelly and her mom wait for us in the front yard.

"Are you taking care of that baby?" Auntie Bernadette asks before she's completely out of the car. I want to steer her away from Mrs. Johnson's stomach, but it's too late.

"Ah," Auntie Bernadette says, placing her hand on Mrs. Johnson's pumpkin pouch, "this boy is doing nicely. He's a big boy."

I hold my breath, but Mary Kelly's mom smiles. "Bernadette, won't you come in for a glass of iced tea?"

No, say no, I pray.

"How nice." Auntie Bernadette glances at me.

I shoot a sharp look her way.

"That's so kind of you to ask me, but I have to hurry back so that I can make dinner for Isabel's family."

I should be relieved, but instead, I feel a twinge of guilt about being embarrassed of my auntie. If she'd only keep her mouth shut and her good hand to herself.

Treasures fill Mary Kelly's house, treasures from the places they've traveled to. A framed red kimono from Japan, a model of a navy ship from Norfolk, a barrel filled with wooden canes from Tennessee.

Mrs. Johnson offers me a chocolate chip cookie fresh from the oven. Mary Kelly's home is like those in an old TV show, a mom in the kitchen with cookies made from scratch.

"They're not homemade," Mary Kelly says. "She scoops the cookie dough out of a plastic container." Mary Kelly's mom sighs and walks out of the kitchen.

When Tonya and Delia arrive, they act shy and quiet, instead of being filled with their usual noisy chatter. Maybe the Johnsons' fine things make them feel like they're on a different island.

Mary Kelly gives us a tour of her house. "This is where the brat will sleep." She points to a pink room and the crib filled with lacy bedding. Olivia's face flashes in my mind. I hope she remembers to go to the bathroom before bedtime.

Mary Kelly's room is next door to the baby's room. "I'll have to wear earplugs at night," she tells us.

A yellow floral Hawaiian quilt covers her bed and stuffed animals are piled high in a corner. The largest collection of Madame Alexander dolls that I've ever seen crowds on the top shelf of a tall bookcase. The lower shelves are crammed with books. She even owns a leather copy of *Jane Eyre*. A blue diary with a tiny lock sits on top of the desk next to her bed.

Mary Kelly is wrong. *This* is the brat's room.

Bathing Suit Switch

Mary Kelly opens a dresser drawer and pulls out eight bathing suits—eight *one-piece* bathing suits. "Borrow one of mine," she says, and it doesn't sound like an offer at all. It sounds like an order.

Even though we've brought our suits, Delia and Tonya pick one of Mary Kelly's. Delia selects an orange one, Tonya green. Mary Kelly looks at me, waiting. I ignore the suits on the bed, go into the bathroom, and return five minutes later, wearing my bikini.

A Thousand Miles Away

Mary Kelly's father drives us to the pool. Dr. Johnson looks so different than Tata, tall and blond, but something about him reminds me of my father. Maybe the way he seems to listen to something else instead of Mary Kelly, who tells him about Sister Rachel's thick ankles and enormous calves. "Her whole body is skinny except for her lower legs. What makes them huge like stuffed sausages?" Her father focuses ahead, not even noticing that she's asked him a question.

"Dad? Why are her legs like that?"

"Hmmm?"

Mary Kelly snaps her tongue against the roof of her mouth and stares out the window. She seems to have forgotten we're here. She turns toward us and rolls her eyes. "The absentminded doctor!"

Delia and Tonya giggle. But I'm thinking how Dr. Johnson's head is so busy, he can't see the man's class ring hanging around his daughter's neck.

No Tom Cruise

Mary Kelly's Mike is no movie star. He's tiny, with deep ruts on his red face from acne. He likes to stare at other girls. He likes to look at my belly button.

Delia flirts with Mike, giggling at his stupid movie star impressions. But Tonya and I climb off the sundeck and go down to the pool. Tonya keeps pulling at the seat of her borrowed swimsuit. Mary Kelly must be two sizes smaller than her. She walks quickly to the water, probably to hide her exposed cheeks.

Even though I've never dived before, I pass up the low diving board and wait in line for the highest one. When it's my turn, I climb the ladder, walk quickly to the edge of the board, and dive before I can change my mind. My body drops through the air and soars through the cold water.

For a moment I forget who I am, and the water and I become one.

Tonya swims over to me. "Hey, you're good at that. Where did you learn to dive?"

I shrug, swim to the side of the pool, climb out, and dive again and again.

The Power of Chocolate

After supper, we talk about everything we can possibly talk about—Mike, the sisters, who we think is cute at school. We play four rounds of truth or dare, double dare, promise or repeat. We eat two giant bowls of popcorn and a supersized bag of M&M's.

One by one, they fall asleep. Delia sleeps next to Mary Kelly in her bed. Tonya snores in a sleeping bag next to me. I listen to the big clock, ticking in the hall. The clock chimes twice; then, an hour later, three times. I get up and walk down the hall.

Mrs. Johnson paces back and forth in the living room, her hand on the small of her back. She gasps when she sees me staring at her a few yards away. "Oh, Isabel. You scared me. Are you okay?"

"I couldn't sleep."

"Me either. Come on," she says, leading me to the kitchen.

A few moments later we're sitting at the table with mugs of hot chocolate and chocolate chip cookies. "There's nothing that chocolate can't cure," she says. And sitting there across from her in the dim light, I believe her. I want to stuff myself with chocolate and let my head clear.

"I'm so glad that Mary Kelly has made some nice friends here. It was such a relief to her father and me when we found a good Catholic school with the same program as the last school she attended."

I nod like I already knew why Mary Kelly went to St. Cletus instead of the base school.

"Is Mike nice?" she asks.

I must look surprised because she quickly adds, "Yes, I know about him. Mothers know everything that goes on with their children."

Maybe some mothers, I think.

"He seems nice enough," I say.

"He's too old for her, but I know Mary Kelly. She bores easily. I won't have to break it off. And if I did, she'd be determined to keep seeing him." She looks down and rests her hand on her stomach. "I'm afraid Mary Kelly isn't too thrilled about this baby."

I push the crumbs around my plate, not wanting to give anything away, not wanting to hurt her with the truth.

We're silent for a while. I glance around the kitchen. On the counter a wooden block holds some steak knives. I think of Frank and a shiver runs down my back. When I shudder, Mrs. Johnson asks, "Are you cold?"

I shake my head. The quiet returns, and I know I should go to bed and let Mrs. Johnson get some sleep, but I like being with her. Then she asks, "Isabel, I hope you don't mind me asking, but how did your mother die?"

I study her face and realize she doesn't know. And instead of saying the things I'd planned to say if anyone ever asked—my mother had a heart attack, she had cancer, she was murdered, instead of all those things, I say, "My mother killed herself."

A deep breath escapes Mrs. Johnson's mouth. She reaches across the table and grabs my hand.

Good-bye

This morning, I'm the last to be picked up. Auntie Bernadette, again, refuses Mrs. Johnson's offer for iced tea. Today I wish she'd accept.

"Isabel must tend to the store and I have my customers to see."

Mary Kelly says, "Good-bye. See you Monday."

But it's Mrs. Johnson that I don't want to say good-bye to.

And when she puts her arm around me and tells Auntie Bernadette, "We like this girl. We want to keep her," I squeeze every bad thought out of my head and wish with all my might that what Mrs. Johnson says could be true.

Secrets

Teresita drops by the cabana. "I invited Frank to the movie. Even Roman asked him, but he didn't want to go. Roman said Frank has been acting *kaduku*."

"Roman needs to mind his own business."

"How did he get those scars on his knee?"

"He's a boy. Boys get scrapes and bruises." Even I'm surprised to hear the anger in my voice.

"Just asking," Teresita says. "You sound like there's some big secret."

"How many tickets have you sold?"

"I have no idea," she says. Every day that passes, she gets grumpier. "I haven't counted."

I don't believe Teresita. It's a few days before the fiesta, and most of the girls share their total sales even though they're not supposed to.

Everyone speculates, even my father.

"You think Teresita might win?" he asks me later.

"I don't know," I say. "Might as well be her as anybody else."

Tata buys a couple of tickets every week from Teresita. Maybe he feels sorry for her.

Breaking Up

Mary Kelly broke up with Mike last night and at recess we have to hear the gritty details—how he called too much, how he wanted to know her every move, how he was a terrible kisser. Mrs. Johnson was right, but did she know Mary Kelly's breakup would be this soon?

"He wasn't that cute," Delia says.

"Yeah, you can do better than him," says Tonya.

I yawn. "Broke up with you because you wouldn't have sex, huh?"

Delia and Tonya stare at me with wide eyes. "Isabel!"

Mary Kelly lowers her eyebrows. "I broke up with *him*! What made you say that anyway?"

"I don't know. He's eighteen. Older boys want more than most girls your age will give out."

Mary Kelly pushes my knee away from her reach. "Most girls my age? I'm your age. You act like you're so grown-up, like you're my mother. And I don't need another mother. I don't even want the one I have."

Everything happens so fast. Suddenly, I'm in front of Sister Rachel again. This time, I'm trying to explain the red mark on Mary Kelly's cheek.

Nice Girls

"What happened to you?" Tata asks me. "You used to be such a nice girl."

Nice girls don't smack their friend's face.

Nice girls don't get disapproving looks from their aunties.

Nice girls don't have to clean the school's toilets after class.

Swimming

*O*livia wants to go swimming. So at five o'clock, I close the store, change into my swimsuit, and take her to the village pool. Wearing his mirrored sunglasses, the unofficial lifeguard, Benny, sits in a lawn chair. He's the official janitor for the mayor's office. Since the pool is next to the mayor's office, the mayor asked if, between mopping floors and cleaning toilets, Benny could keep an eye on the swimmers. I don't even know if Benny can swim. I've never seen him in the pool.

Mrs. Cruz sits under a big umbrella, watching John Wayne jump up and down in the water.

I stand with my legs apart in the pool and Olivia swims between them. She's able to do that three times before coming up for air. The water feels good, not too cold, not too hot. I remember the other night when I dived off the high board at the base pool. I loved that feeling of freedom when my body met the water, the cool sensation, and the hollow sound beneath the surface. Underwater, my worries disappear. I don't think about Mary Kelly or Frank.

John Wayne comes over to us. "Can I play, too?" he asks.

"Sure," I say. I wouldn't want just any thirteen-year-old guy to swim between my legs, but John Wayne isn't like any thirteen-year-old guy.

"Isabel," Mrs. Cruz calls out, "I'm still waiting for you to come by."

"I know. I will . . . soon," I lie.

Before we leave, I tell Benny, "You need to get the mayor to add a diving board to the pool."

"It's too shallow," he says. "You'd crack your head open and then you'd be an idiot."

I try hard not to look at Mrs. Cruz, but out of the corner of my eye, I notice her flinch.

Preparations

The fiesta is this coming weekend. Olivia and I pass the preparations as we walk back home from the pool.

Tata is helping some of the other men set up the big white tents for bingo, cockfights, and other games. The food concession stands are already lined up on the side of the road, empty and waiting for action. A blue crepe paper skirt surrounds the pageant stage. Tomorrow the kiddy rides will arrive and Malesso will look like the circus has come to town.

Olivia releases my hand and skips ahead of me, singing, "I can't wait till fiesta! Fiesta! Fiesta!" When I was her age, I must have felt the same way. I must have.

Sorry

Auntie Bernadette oversleeps on Wednesday and we are fifteen minutes late for school. Walking into class late will be bad enough, but I run into Mrs. Johnson on the way.

I stare down at the sidewalk and hope she doesn't see me, but Mrs. Johnson stops when I pass her.

"Isabel." Her voice is soft and when I turn, I notice her face is, too. "Is there anything bothering you?"

I try to swallow the lump in my throat. "No. I'm . . . I'm sorry about Mary Kelly. I didn't . . . mean—"

Mrs. Johnson puts her hand on my arm. "Of course not. Don't get me wrong, I hope it doesn't happen again, but I feel like I got to know you a little the other night. Mary Kelly must have said something terribly hurtful to cause you to do that."

Mrs. Johnson waits. She must want me to tell her what Mary Kelly said, but I look away. I feel like I got to know Mrs. Johnson the other night, too, and I wouldn't hurt her for a million dollars.

"Isabel, would you do me a favor?"

Anything, I think. Anything to get rid of this miserable guilt hanging around my neck like a heavy chain.

"Would you ask Mary Kelly to the fiesta this weekend?"

Anything but that.

Surprises

Mrs. Johnson says Mary Kelly will say yes. "Just you watch. I know she values your friendship. And anyway, if you let what happened fester, it will become worse than it really is."

Mrs. Johnson may have been right about Mary Kelly breaking up with Mike, but she's wrong about this.

"Isabel, I know that it's none of my business, but did you talk to anyone after your mother died?"

"What do you mean?"

"A counselor or a therapist?"

I hug my books close to my chest. "Mrs. Johnson, I'm late for school. I need to hurry." I walk away quickly but add, "I promise to ask Mary Kelly."

All morning, Mary Kelly ignores me, never looking my way. Even Tonya and Delia act differently toward me, giving short answers to my questions. I want to forget my promise to Mrs. Johnson and make new friends. But after a quick look around, I realize these are the only people I want to be my friends.

At lunch I race past a few girls in order to get in line right behind Mary Kelly. I blurt the question out so fast that it sounds like, "Would you like golden mustard this weekend?"

"What?" she asks with a funny scowl.

I repeat the words slower. "Would you like to go to the Malesso fiesta this weekend?" Then I hold my breath.

"Maybe," Mary Kelly says. "If I'm not busy."

I'm so shocked, it takes me a moment to notice the cafeteria lady holding out my carton of chocolate milk.

List for Fiesta Preparations

1. Slice eggplant
2. Gather the *achiote* seeds for Auntie's red rice
3. Call Auntie Minerva and ask her to bring her chicken *kelaguen* (Tata's request, not mine)
4. Order plenty of *tuba* from Roman's dad
5. ~~Ask Frank to~~ chop onions

Morning of the Pageant

The morning of the pageant, Teresita calls me at six. "Why didn't you tell me I was a fool to run for queen?"

"You made up your mind without me. And no one changes your mind, Teresita."

"I've thrown up twice this morning and I haven't even eaten anything."

Now I feel sorry for her. If it was someone like Olivia, who dreamed of being queen her whole life, I'd ignore her, but Teresita running for queen is like a fish trying to grow legs.

The Legend of Sirena

My favorite legend is the one about Sirena. I don't know if it's my favorite because I love the story or because it's the only legend that my father told me. When I was younger, I wanted to be special in Tata's eyes. Every day I waited for him to return from the sea. Usually he was too busy cleaning fish to give me much attention, but one day when I was six, he told me about a girl named Sirena who lived in Agana during the Spanish times on Guam.

Sirena loved to swim in the fresh spring waters where the Minondo River met the ocean. She loved to swim so much that sometimes she skipped her chores and headed for the water.

One day her mother sent her to gather coconut shells to heat the iron. The river beckoned to her and she swam while her mother called her name. Her mother knew where her daughter must be and she angrily cursed her.

"Since Sirena loves the water so much, she should become a fish."

Sirena never returned home because she soon discovered that from the waist down, she'd become a fish. To this day she is said to be swimming in the Pacific Ocean. Many fishermen have reported seeing her over the years.

When I asked Tata if he'd ever seen her, he said, "Oh, yes. Many times." He winked and patted my head. "She even knows my name. 'Hey, Vincent,' she says, 'how's the fishing?' I tell her to come closer, but she can only be caught with a net of human hair."

Since my father was a master at making fishing nets, I begged him to make one with my hair. He just laughed.

Someone Else

When Olivia twirls to breakfast in her fanciest church dress, I tell her to change to shorts.

"But I'm going to the queen's pageant!" she says.

"You're not in the pageant. And it's hot outside."

She doesn't budge.

"You won't get to eat a snow cone."

The thought of missing out on a sour grape snow cone does the trick. She returns three minutes later dressed in her denim shorts and blue top.

Tata walks inside the house. "Where's that tablecloth your mo . . . where's the tablecloth we use for fiesta?"

He almost sounds like the old Tata, trying to take care of things. I open a drawer near the sink and dig out the red tablecloth we use to cover the picnic table for barbecues and fiestas.

"The iceman was supposed to come yesterday," Tata says. "Give him a call, okay? Jesus, everybody is going to want ice today. Of all days for him not to show up!"

Hearing Tata gripe makes me feel so good for some reason.

There's a knock at the door and I know it must be Mary Kelly. Olivia has hardly eaten the eggs I've scrambled, and Frank hasn't even made it to the table.

"Olivia, answer the door while I get Frank." Now I feel like Tata—of all days for Frank to sleep in.

Frank's room is dark and he's curled in a ball under his sheet. Two glassy eyes stare out at me.

"Come on, Frank! Today is fiesta! Don't you want to have fun?"

"I'm sleepy. I'll be over later." He covers his face.

I think of forcing him out of bed, but Mary Kelly's voice pulls me away. For once, just for today, I'll forget about Frank. I'll have fun at fiesta with my friend. I'll cheer for a contestant in the queen's pageant, play silly games at every booth, cha-cha to the music. Just for today.

Primping

We play games, eat snow cones, and watch Olivia take eight turns on the Tilt-A-Twirl. But we're like everyone else, waiting for the queen's court to prance across the stage. Thirty minutes to go.

Until then we watch the contestants do their final touches. Lipsticks glide across lips. Powder puffs pat noses. Hair spray fumes fill the air.

While the rest of the court primps, Teresita sits on a Coca-Cola case, frowning. The hem of her blue dress puddles at her feet. Auntie Bernadette nears her with a comb, but Teresita jerks back and shakes her head. "Enough!"

"Who is she?" asks Mary Kelly.

Teresita looks beautiful. Long hair flowing past her shoulders, practically touching the ground. The makeup she wears magnifies her brown eyes, and I realize now why the boys melt in front of her, even when she cusses them out.

"Who is she, Isabel?" Mary Kelly repeats.

"Teresita," Olivia says. "And she's going to win."

"She couldn't care less about being queen," I say.

"Sure," Mary Kelly says. "Why would she run, then?"

"It's complicated," I tell her.

Auntie Bernadette lifts Teresita's hem. When women walk by and admire the blue dress, she smiles proudly. "Yes, I made it. But Teresita would make burlap look like satin."

My cheeks sting. I don't even know why. It's just a prissy blue dress and a stupid contest.

"If you ask me," Mary Kelly says, staring at Teresita, "that girl wants to be queen."

A Familiar Face

A woman with a familiar face stands between Teresita's auntie and uncle. Finally I realize she's Teresita's mother.

The last time I saw her was three years ago, standing in Teresita's auntie's yard. She was skinny and high as the moon. On the side of the road, her boyfriend waited in his old truck with the missing passenger door. Teresita's auntie was pulling on Teresita's right arm while her mother yanked the left. I thought she was going to split down the middle until they each had half.

Teresita didn't make a sound. Her face paled and her body went limp like a rag doll's. Teresita's mom let go of her arm and grabbed Teresita's hair, crying, "You're coming with me."

The color returned to Teresita's face and her arm shook loose of her auntie's grasp. Then she shoved her mother and yelled, "Go away and leave me alone. I don't want to ever see you again."

By then, neighbors were watching from their windows and doorways. The brave ones had moved closer to the yard for a first-row view. Her mother stood and stared at Teresita a long moment. Teresita and her mother had a stare down. Teresita won. Her mother staggered away to her boyfriend's truck. She didn't even have the satisfaction of slamming a door since it was missing. They drove away, leaving Teresita kneeling on the grass and her auntie making the sign of the cross.

But today I watch Teresita looking at her mother from the stage, and I can tell that she has forgotten she used to curse her mother's name.

Queen

The mayor is about to announce the queen and Teresita is one of two girls remaining. Forget the chickens! I want to grab her by the hand and take off for Cocos Island.

"The winner sold thirty thousand tickets this year," the mayor says, and when he calls Teresita's name for the winner, she lets out a little squeal and puts her hand to her mouth and tears well up in her eyes. She trembles as last year's queen pins the tiara to her head and slips the banner across her chest. Teresita glides down the stage and waves with a big beauty queen smile.

Her mother and auntie hug each other and smile at the girl on the stage with the crown on her head. I can't believe my eyes.

"See," Mary Kelly says. "Told you she wanted to be queen."

Auntie Bernadette beams as if the dress is the reason Teresita won instead of the number of tickets we sold. Did she act like this when my mother won?

Olivia jumps and jumps.

Roman lightly punches my shoulder. "This is another lucky sign!"

I hope he wins the three hundred cans of tuna. And Teresita, instead of the great escape I'd planned for her, I want to slap her all the way to the Miss Universe contest.

Queen's Ball

The queen and her royal court get twelve invitations each to go to the Queen's Ball, held right after the pageant. Teresita gave me enough for my family and Mary Kelly. I'll go, though I don't want to, but I made the mistake of telling Mary Kelly earlier and now she's dying to go.

The Queen's Ball is held in the community center. Auntie Bernadette is there, and Teresita's auntie and uncle. I'm surprised to see Roman there as well. I guess he showed up for the drawing at the end of the ball.

People gather around Teresita, congratulating her. She hugs them all, lets the men kiss her on the cheek, and tells everyone, "Thank you. Thank you for buying my tickets." Her mother sits across the room, smiling and watching Teresita and her admirers. She hardly looks like the woman staggering around Teresita's yard a few years ago.

Auntie Bernadette acts like a proud momma when

the women go on and on about the dress. "It was noth-ing," she says. "So simple to make. You hardly notice the dress with Teresita's beauty."

I'm relieved a lot of people surround Teresita because I won't have to say anything to her.

Mary Kelly throws me a bewildered expression. "I thought you said Teresita was a cockfighter."

I shake my head. "That's not Teresita. I don't know *that* girl."

Cha-cha

$\mathcal{E}$very Chamorro knows the cha-cha. We learn it in our mother's womb.

Teresita dances with her uncle and the royal court dances with their fathers. Even Olivia dances with the younger kids. I think of Tata, who could do the cha-cha better than anyone. He moved the floor when he danced. I look around the room for him, but he's nowhere to be found.

Roman heads in my direction and I'm ready to tell him no. I raise my chin and squint at him. But he holds out his hands to Mary Kelly and Mary Kelly says yes. I'm beginning to wonder if I know my friends at all.

The Great Escape

At one o'clock the men disappear from the room. The cockfight begins in thirty minutes and bets must be made.

Teresita comes over. "You have to sneak me out of here, Isabel."

Two minutes ago, I'd figured out what I was going to tell her. I'd planned to say, "You sure seem to enjoy yourself as queen, Teresita. You're eating it up like ice cream, slurping down every drop."

But now with her facing me, she looks silly. The tiara is sliding off her head; the blue dress suddenly looks like a cheap Halloween costume. I grab her hand. "Come on."

We slip through the kitchen and out the back door. As we near the church, Mary Kelly and Roman catch up with us. "Isabel," Roman says, "I won second prize! A thousand dollars!"

Cockfight

We follow Teresita as she tears through the crowd, making her way to the pit. People are still placing bets, their fingers flying in the air. At the Dededo dome fingers point down, meaning thousands of dollars, fingers to the side, hundreds, but at fiesta fights fingers are straight up, small-time bets. That's why the old people like fiesta cockfights best.

Lorenzo stands in the center, holding Teresita's prize chicken. He startles when he sees Teresita step forward.

"I'll take that chicken from here."

"Go to your ball, pretty one."

"I won the bet. You said if I ran for queen and won, I could have my chickens back."

Lorenzo holds the white chicken away from Teresita's reaching arms. "Get away, little girl."

The mayor emerges from the crowd. He likes a good cockfight as much as any of the other men. "Is this true, Lorenzo?" he asks.

"She's a silly girl, Mayor. Who are you going to believe?"

It's the wrong question to ask the mayor. Everyone knows Lorenzo would pinch a chicken's behind during a fight, causing it to become more feisty and win. And before the mayor was mayor, he lost a few games because of Lorenzo's dirty tricks.

Many people had. Some are here today. So now the crowd begins to shout, "Give the queen her chicken! Give the queen her chicken!"

Even though we stand under an open-sided tent, the crowd steps forward, creating a wall. Finally Lorenzo hands over the chicken to Teresita. "Who wants her lazy chicken anyway?" Leaving the pit, he breaks through the crowd.

Teresita calls after him, "I want all my chickens back, Lorenzo. Remember you promised." Now she isn't worried. She has a hundred witnesses.

Teresita hikes up her blue dress and puts the chicken between her legs. Her tiara falls off. She picks up the rhinestone crown and tosses it to me. "Give it to Olivia."

The referee steps forward and checks the four-inch knife attached to one of the chicken's legs. No one usually cheats at a fiesta fight, but occasionally at the dome there's poison on the knife or sometimes someone will replace the knife with a rubber one.

Teresita ruffles the feathers of her chicken and lets the chicken of the man waiting for the next round peck at her chicken's head and body. This gets the chickens worked up.

"Ready?" the referee asks.

Teresita shakes her opponent's hand.

"Go ahead," the referee yells. A few seconds later the chickens meet in midair and slash at each other.

They hit the dirt floor. Teresita's white chicken flies up, lands on the red chicken, and stabs it with his knife.

The referee jumps in and picks up the birds by their tail feathers.

The red chicken tries to peck Teresita's bird, but the white chicken slashes him again. The red one flops to the ground. Blood spatters.

The referee lifts the chickens. Teresita's bird pecks, pecks, pecks at the red one until it flops in the puddle of blood. The crowd yells. Some cheer. Some groan.

Wallets open and money goes up the crowd and down, like a wave. High over her head, Teresita holds up her chicken, paying no mind to the blood trickling down her arm and onto her blue dress. A two-victory day!

A loud groan escapes the crowd. Auntie Bernadette has made her way to the front. Olivia is right behind her.

Beads of sweat prickle Auntie's forehead and she's breathing heavily. "The blue dress!"

Dance with Me

A band plays on the pageant stage and hundreds, maybe even a thousand people, sit on the grass, listening. I sit with Olivia, Roman, Mary Kelly, and Teresita. Olivia wears Teresita's tiara, and Teresita has changed into shorts and a T-shirt. She won a hundred dollars from the cockfight, although she can't tell anyone since she's underage.

Lucky, lucky. Everyone around me is lucky today. Is it my turn next?

I study the faces in the crowd, searching for Tata. I haven't seen him all day. My watch says it's three o'clock. He's probably at the house, barbecuing fish for the family fiesta.

Mrs. Cruz passes by the stage. John Wayne follows her, dragging a little red wagon behind him. Inside the wagon are boxes that say Star-Kist Tuna. Mrs. Cruz bought only two tickets, but they were lucky. She won a prize anyway.

A few brave couples start to dance in front of the stage.

"Come on, Olivia," Mary Kelly says. "Let's dance. I learned how to cha-cha today."

Olivia takes Mary Kelly's hand and they walk closer to the stage.

Roman yawns and stretches his arms above his head. He peers at me out of the corners of his eyes. "Want to dance?" he asks.

I don't answer. I just stand and let my feet do the talking. One, two, cha-cha-cha.

Food and Family

We leave the village celebration to go home to our families' fiestas. Teresita walks with her mom to her auntie's home and Roman takes off for his house.

Today will be like Christmas, with the special food, music, and family. Auntie Minerva will be there, along with Uncle Fernando and Auntie Bernadette. And Tata's other brothers and sisters and my cousins from the village of Barrigada. Auntie Bernadette even invited Mary Kelly's family. Strangers from around the island will wander into our yard and our neighbors' for plates of food or drinks. "Want some more?" we'll ask. "Take a plate with you." At fiesta everybody is our friend. It's the Guam way.

Fiesta

A line of people has formed by the cabana. On the table there is *pancet*, red rice, frittata, and all the food I love—the dishes served at every fiesta, wedding, christening, and rosary, except *golai hagun sune*. Auntie Minerva doesn't bring her dry chicken *kelaguen*. She brings her dry shrimp *kelaguen*. Auntie Bernadette brings *lumpia, fanihe,* and tamales.

Near the cabana Tata barbecues fish. Mrs. Cruz, Ana, Carmella, and Dominic head our way. Dr. and Mrs. Johnson arrive with a white box filled with pink strawberry cupcakes.

My cousin Hernando plays his guitar, and Olivia dances to the beat. I wish today could last forever.

For a moment, I wonder where Frank is, but I quickly push the thought away.

Right as I finish filling my plate, Auntie Bernadette runs from our house, her good hand waving high in the air. "Vincent, come quick!" she yells.

And I know before she says it that it's Frank.

I Hat

Razor blade on the floor.
Frank asleep.
Asleep?
"I h-a-t" carved in his arm.
No "e."
No "y-o-u."
Blood on his bed,
On his floor,
On his arm.
Son! cries Tata.
Dr. Johnson plays doctor.
What's wrong? we ask.
What's wrong? we cry.
Call 911.
The ambulance from Talofofo arrives
and carries Frank away.
Tata and Dr. Johnson follow.

We stare at the road
even after the ambulance and truck disappear.
Now who is going to eat
besides the flies
circling the fiesta table?

Who Knew?

Everyone waits by the phone. Olivia won't leave my side. And Auntie Minerva keeps making the sign of the cross and asks me questions. "Isabel, did you know about the words on the wall? Did you know about the scars? Did you tell your father?"

Did you?

Did you?

Did you?

I say nothing. Finally Auntie Bernadette says, "Minerva, shut up!"

And for one tiny fleeting moment, I feel good.

Time

The procession for San Dimas will start at dusk, but we won't go. We wait for Tata to return with news about Frank. Mary Kelly and her mother left an hour ago. They left their pink cupcakes behind. Before leaving, Mrs. Johnson grabbed my arm and said, "If you need to talk, call me."

Mary Kelly whispered, "I'm so sorry," then closed the door. I wanted to open the door and run behind them. *Take me with you.*

Later, Teresita drops by and puts her arm around my shoulders. She's never done that before.

"Why aren't you at the church?" I ask her. "The procession will start soon."

"It's a two-block walk around the village."

"But everyone will want another look at the queen."

She lifts her left eyebrow and rolls her eyes. A few hours ago I wanted to ask her why she acted so silly when she was crowned. It was a big deal then. Now it means nothing. The pageant seems like a year ago. How can time do that? One moment flies by so quickly. Another moment stands still.

Bleach

Auntie Bernadette throws Frank's sheets away, but the blood leaves a red spot on the mattress. "Isabel," Auntie says, "help me get this mattress outside."

Teresita, Auntie, and I drag the mattress into the backyard, not the front, where everyone can see our shame. Auntie Bernadette scrubs the spot with bleach and water. Red fades to pink.

She sighs and throws down the sponge. "It's too late."

Too late for what? Too late for the mattress or too late for Frank?

Clean Slate

Tata comes home with a Kmart sack and a pail of paint that matches the color of Frank's walls. He looks our way, not saying a word. And when he sees Teresita, he frowns at me. He probably thinks our shame should stay inside our house, not seep into the village.

Olivia rushes up to Tata. "Where's Frank?"

Tata doesn't turn around. "Go play." He disappears into Frank's room.

Auntie Bernadette motions Olivia over and holds her close.

Soon we hear the *shoo-sa, shoo-sa, shoo-sa* of the sandpaper riding up and down Frank's wall.

Unraveling

When Tata doesn't come out of the room to tell us about Frank, Auntie Bernadette goes to Tata.

The sanding stops for a while. I hear their voices, but I can't make out their words until Tata says, "No." And the sanding begins again.

Auntie Bernadette comes out of the room. "Let's take a walk to the pier," she tells us. "Teresita, you better go home now."

Teresita, who is not used to anyone telling her what to do, touches my arm. "Bye. I hope Frank is okay."

My heart beats fast against my chest. Beads of sweat roll down my face. Olivia and I follow my auntie down the road. We reach the pier, but Auntie Bernadette keeps walking. People pour out of the church and line up for the procession around the village. The parishioners are in front with the cart that carries the statue of San Dimas. The priests and choirboys are next, followed by the village people.

We're having our own parade—Auntie leading the way, Olivia trailing behind me. At the park, Auntie Bernadette stops and turns my way. I'm not ready to hear what Tata told Auntie Bernadette in Frank's room.

"Isabel," Auntie says, "the doctor says Frank's counselor will probably want to talk with you and Olivia."

I squeeze Olivia's hand. I can't bear to hear that my brother is dead from someone who didn't know him. "Can't you tell me?"

"Tell you what? He wants to ask you questions."

"But Frank . . . what about Frank? Why do we have to answer questions now?"

The two lines between Auntie's eyebrows soften and she puts her arm around me. "Oh, Isabel, did you think . . . ?" She glances at Olivia, who keeps looking toward the fiesta rides. "Oh, no. No. Frank is fine. Well, not fine, but he's going to be all right."

My knees relax and my whole body wants to collapse. I drop Olivia's sweaty hand and hug my little sister tight.

She wiggles free. "Isabel, can I go on the Tilt-A-Twirl tonight?"

The Morning After

I pick up my notebook to write today's list, but the words won't come.

My Fault

Frank's counselor wants to have family sessions but thinks it's important to meet with us one-on-one first. Tata won't go. Maybe Tata thought he fixed the problem by painting Frank's wall.

I don't want to go either, but I will for Frank. I'll tell them what they want to know—that I saw the words on Frank's walls, saw the scars on Frank's arms, and said nothing. So now they will know who to blame.

Back to School

Delia and Tonya whisper to each other but never mention Frank. Do they know? If they do, why don't they say so? Why do they move about like they're trying not to bump into any furniture? Like mentioning Frank's name will break me?

By lunch, I'm so mad, I glare at them and say, "I just started my period last month. I wear sanitary napkins and I don't douche!" Sometimes the truth feels like a weapon.

Mary Kelly wasn't in school today. I can't help but think her absence might have something to do with what happened on Saturday. Sunday, when I answered the phone, I was disappointed that it was Dr. Johnson who called to check on Frank, not Mrs. Johnson. Maybe she thinks we're too *kaduka* for her smart haole family. Maybe she's right.

Do Not Enter

After school Monday, Auntie Bernadette drives us to the hospital. She says she'll visit Frank on the patients' wing while Olivia and I visit the counselor. But the nurse at the desk says Frank can't have a visitor yet.

"Not even his favorite auntie?" Auntie Bernadette asks.

"Sorry," the nurse says, but she doesn't even look up from her computer.

"When may I see him?"

"The doctor will let you know."

I study the huge gray double doors that say VISITORS MUST CHECK IN AT THE DESK BEFORE ENTERING.

Five minutes later a Filipino lady dressed in floral scrubs walks through another door. "Olivia Moreno."

Auntie and I both stand to go with her. The lady smiles. "Sorry, you'll need to wait here. Don't worry, she'll be okay."

I grit my teeth. What right do these strangers have to build boundaries around my sister and brother?

Olivia takes the woman's hand and goes with her without as much as a glimpse back. It bothers me that my sister lets people in her life as easily as a key slips through a keyhole.

Walk This Way

Olivia returns thirty minutes later, smiling, with a pack of chewing gum. "I drew pictures," she says, smacking her gum.

"Isabel," the lady says. "Please follow me."

With each step down the long white hall the words sound off in my head. *I knew. I knew. I knew.*

Introductions

The counselor is not the Filipino lady. The counselor is a fat Chamorro man. At his desk, he's eating the last bite of a hamburger. Wiping off his mouth with a napkin, he motions me in, stands, and holds out his hand. "I'm Eduardo Gurrero. Just call me, Ed, though."

I take his hand, then quickly release it.

"Sorry about the mess," he says, wadding up his McDonald's sack and throwing it into the garbage. "That was a late lunch. I have to squeeze my meals in between sessions."

His office is a mess. There are supersized McDonald's cups around the room, five that I've counted so far. Books are crammed on shelves and stacked in towers on his floor. Animal puppets lie in a pile on his chair. An old poster I've seen in movies is tacked to the wall. It's the one with the pretty lady wearing the red bathing suit, but someone has made a muumuu for her, covering almost everything from the neck down.

"Isabel, I guess you were in school today?"

I'm wearing my uniform, but I politely say, "Yes."

"Where do you attend school?"

"St. Cletus." I glance down to make sure I'm wearing the white blouse embroidered with my school's name.

"Of course, of course." He leans back in his chair. It squeaks and I wonder if it will break from his heavy body. He gets up, walks around away from the desk, and somehow manages to get to the couch without tipping over any books.

Ed flops on the couch and locks his hands behind his neck. "Well, I understand you're the oldest. I guess that means you have a lot of responsibilities?"

Here it is. I might as well get it over. I breathe deep and say, "It's my fault. I knew about Frank."

Ed appears confused. "What do you mean, it's your fault?"

"I knew Frank was hurting himself, at least I thought he might be. I w-wasn't sure, but I should h—"

Ed holds up his palm. "Whoa, whoa, Isabel. We're not here to talk about Frank."

"We're not?"

"We're here to talk about you."

"But I thought I was here to help Frank."

"I'd like to know more about you first."

"I don't need help."

"Maybe not, but why don't we just explore a few things. For instance, what's life been like for you since your mother died?"

I bite the inside of my cheeks and fold my arms in front of my chest. I look at the girl in the poster; I count McDonald's cups. There are seven. I imagine the puppets dancing the cha-cha around the room. I don't say another word.

Tick Tock

Time drags when two people face each other and don't say anything. Ed tries. He asks about school. He asks about Auntie and living in Malesso.

Do I know Mrs. Cruz, the fish artist? He tells me he bought a picture from her last year. He points to the painting of the skipjack over the couch.

Ed's plan doesn't work. I won't even move my lips because I know his questions will lead back to one thing—my mother.

No Crayons

"What did you draw?" Olivia asks me on the ride back home.

"I didn't draw anything."

"I drew Auntie, Mommy, Tata, Frank, and you. I even drew Ed. But I made him skinny. I didn't want him to be sad."

"I hope you didn't want me to feel sad, too," says Auntie.

Sticks and Stones

Roman stops by the cabana. "How's Frank?"

And just that one question is like the last drop in a full bathtub that makes the water run over the rim.

"Why do you want to know? You don't care about Frank. If you did, you wouldn't steal my father away from him."

Roman picks up his fishing pole and walks away. My stomach aches as I watch him head home.

Sticks and stones will break my bones, but words will never hurt me.

I don't believe that playground saying.

Mistaken Identity

After supper, Mary Kelly calls me. "How's your brother?"

"Fine," I say, though I don't know. Tata didn't even ask if we'd seen him when we got home. But he made hamburgers.

"That's good," Mary Kelly says. "Guess what?" Her voice changes and she sounds cheerful.

Her sudden happiness irritates me. Still, I ask, "What?"

"My mother had the baby Sunday."

Maybe that's why Mrs. Johnson didn't call. Maybe she was going into labor.

"And your aunt was right. He's a boy!"

"He is?" Auntie all of a sudden seems like the smartest person in the world.

"Yep, the hospital must have gotten the test mixed up with someone else's. Maybe the other family could switch their blue things for our pink." She laughs. "He's so cute. Mom says he looks like me when I was a baby, blue eyes and white fuzz on top of his head. Maybe you can come to the hospital tomorrow after school. You could see him through the nursery window."

"Maybe," I tell her, but I don't plan to return to any more hospitals.

Show-and-Tell

At school Tuesday, Mary Kelly shows us pictures of her baby brother. Mrs. Johnson let Mary Kelly name him—Matthew Kolby Johnson. "We have the same initials," she says. "I've changed his diaper already. And you know what? His poop doesn't really stink that bad. That's because my mom is breast-feeding him."

Tonya and Delia laugh and shake their heads. Watch out, Mary Kelly. Your little brother won't always be so sweet and perfect. One day he'll be singing and playing the ukulele. Then when you stop looking and listening, the songs will leave and he'll exchange the ukulele for a razor blade.

"He has monkey toes! They're as long as his fingers. So cute," Mary Kelly says.

Watch out, girl.

Confession

Monday arrives and now I have two things to dread, school and my appointment with Ed. "I'm not going to the hospital," I tell Auntie after school.

"I want to go," Olivia says. "Ed said we could play with the puppets again."

"Don't worry, Olivia," Auntie says. "You're going."

We drive to the hospital. A different nurse calls Olivia's name and takes her to Ed.

When they walk away, I ask, "Why didn't you tell the nurse that I'm not going today?"

"Tell her yourself." Auntie picks up a *Redbook* magazine and flips to the recipe section.

I feel as if she slapped me. Auntie never snaps back. She closes the magazine and looks around the waiting room. The only people here are the receptionist and an older lady sitting in the corner. Auntie Bernadette moves to the seat next to me.

"Isabel, you must know something. I haven't had the

words until this moment." She takes a big breath. "I didn't know how to heal her."

"My mom?"

"Yes. I can heal sore throats, fevers, help the scarred wombs of childless women grow babies, but I couldn't heal my little sister. I should have told her to go to the doctor. To a psychiatrist. I couldn't accept my happy beautiful sister ever being sad."

"Why *was* she sad?"

"I don't know. She didn't know either. Once Erlinda told me, 'I see darkness when I want to see light. What's wrong with me?' I told her, 'Play your ukulele, dance in your tiara. No one's looking.'" Auntie's voice cracks and her eyes grow wet. "A fool's advice. I should have known better. I have limits."

I place my hand on top of her good one. "It's not your fault. You can't cure the whole world."

She points her finger at me. "Exactly, Isabel. That's why you need to talk to Dr. Gurrero."

"I don't see how talking to him about me is going to help Frank."

Auntie shrugs. "Maybe it won't. Maybe it will. How will you know if you don't try? I've decided if he wants to talk to me, I'll go." Ed better be ready to listen.

The nurse returns with Olivia and calls my name. And I follow her.

Talking

*E*d's room smells like raw onions, probably from another Big Mac attack. "*Hafa adai*, Isabel," he says. "How are you?"

"Fine."

He walks around, shakes my hand, and leans back against his desk. "It's good to hear you speak. I was beginning to think you had laryngitis last week." He chuckles, then clears his throat when I don't smile.

"Mind if I sit here?" He points to the couch across from me, then plops down. He's wearing a blue Hawaiian shirt today and eyeglasses. I'm trying to remember if he wore the round wire frames last week when he asks, "Anything happen since we talked? I mean since *I* talked?" He chuckles again.

I sigh.

"Sorry. No more jokes. How's school?"

I don't know why, but I say, "My friend's mother had a baby."

"Great! Girl or boy?"

"Boy." I smile, remembering Auntie's prediction, then quickly suck in my lips.

"Why did you do that?"

"Do what?"

"Erase your smile."

"When am I going to see Frank?"

"I'll make a deal with you. You talk to me today and I'll tell you at the end of this session. Okay? Now, why did you wipe off your smile?"

"I don't know. I was thinking about how Auntie Bernadette told Mary Kelly's family their baby would be a boy and they didn't believe her." I explain what happened—how Mrs. Johnson took the test, the test that never fails, the mix-up, the pink nursery, the little pink dresses hanging in the closet.

Ed laughs. "Never underestimate a *suruhana*."

By the end of our session, we haven't talked about much except school and my friends.

"See you next week," Ed says.

"But when can I see Frank?"

"I think he'll be ready for a visit in about two weeks."

"Two weeks? But you said if I talked to you—"

"I said if you talked to me, I'd tell you when you'd be able to see Frank. I told you, two weeks."

"But—"

"See you next week, Isabel."

Steps

"How's your shrink?" Teresita asks. We're sitting in the cabana, waiting for customers.

"He's not my shrink. He's Frank's."

"I've heard of women getting crushes on their shrinks and some even fall hopelessly in love with them."

Before I can explain that Ed isn't my type or maybe not anyone's, John Wayne appears. He's wearing his cowboy hat and holster. But today he also wears black cowboy boots. He crosses the grass toward us, taking long careful steps.

"Howdy, little ladies."

"Howdy, John Wayne," we say.

Teresita whistles. "Looking pretty sharp in those boots, John Wayne."

"They're Tony Lamas," John Wayne says. "Roman bought them for me." My stomach feels queasy, thinking of the other day with Roman.

"That Roman is a pretty cool guy," Teresita says, winking and poking me in the ribs.

I don't want to talk about Roman, so I ask, "How is your mom?"

Teresita grows serious. "She's okay. She wants me to live with her when she's finished with her therapy."

My throat tightens. "In Barrigada?"

"No, here in Malesso. She still owns her house here."

My shoulders drop back in place. I couldn't bear to have another person leave my life.

Consequences

After I feed Olivia supper, I wait for Tata and Roman to return from fishing, but when Tata reaches the cabana with his nets in hand, he's alone.

"Where's Roman?" I ask.

"He didn't show up today. He hasn't fished with me the last few days."

I decide facing Roman is better than the misery I'm feeling. I head to his house. Why do words fall so easily from my mouth but are so hard to take back?

Roman is weeding his mother's flower bed when I walk up.

"How do you know which ones are weeds?" I ask.

"Whichever ones my mother says are." He looks up at me and waits, grinning. Does he know why I'm here?

"Roman, I'm sorry about the other day." I swallow. "I'm just worried about Frank."

He brushes the dirt from his hands and stands. "I know, Isabel. No problem."

A warm feeling rolls over my body like an ocean wave covering the coral reef. He is still smiling with that crooked mouth and it grows cuter by the second.

"I mean if you want to go fishing with Tata, it's okay. I mean . . . I think you should."

He nods and says, "Isabel, you're smiling. Isabel Moreno remembered how to smile."

Empty

Tonight in bed, I touch my lips. They betrayed me twice today. Once in Ed's office and once in front of Roman. I don't want to smile when my brother is in the hospital. I don't want to feel happy, even for one minute, not until Frank is home.

I lie awake and wait for Olivia's nightmare, but one o'clock comes and goes. I walk through the house, stopping by Frank's room. The wall is immaculate. The mattress has been replaced.

My father is asleep on the floor and even though there's a chill in the house, I don't bother to cover him.

Puppet Show

Morning arrives and I realize that Olivia didn't have a nightmare last night. I slide my hand between the sheets, but they're dry.

At breakfast I ask Olivia what she and Ed talked about yesterday.

"We played puppets. Ed pretended the cat puppet was Mommy. And I got to be me, but I was a duck. I told Mommy I missed her."

"Oh?"

"Yeah. And Mommy said she loved me. She hugged me and she said she missed me, too." Olivia drinks the rest of her chocolate milk, then wipes off her wet mustache with the back of her hand.

I don't have the heart to remind her that puppets are make-believe. She's not a duck and our mother was not a cat. A dumb game can't undo all the harm my mother caused by leaving us.

A Gentle Reminder

"You need to carry baby formula," Ana tells me at the store. "For emergencies."

"Don't they have it at the pier store?"

"Nope, just a bunch of stuff the tourists would want—T-shirts, junk food, and lots of film. Japanese people sure take a lot of pictures. They even snap pictures of Carmella and me."

"They used to shop here. Maybe we should have carried more film."

"Have you seen the painting Mom did of your mother?"

I shake my head, a bit embarrassed to admit that I haven't. I wipe a rag over the counter. "My dad let me order more comics. Do you want to see them?"

"Nah, I don't have time for that since I had Carmella." Ana pays for the six-pack of Diet Cokes and heads to the door. She turns toward me and says, "You know, I used to think my mother did the stupidest things, like painting those boring fish and how she lets my brother say he's John Wayne. But now I figured it out. I think she does those silly things because she loves us."

Monday Q&A with Ed

"Tell me about your mother."

"I don't remember her."

"What do you mean?"

"I don't remember what she looks like, smells like, sounds like."

"When did this happen?"

"A couple of months ago. I awoke one morning and didn't remember."

"When you see pictures of her, do you remember?"

"Nope. I mean, I know it's her, but I don't remember her."

"You can't remember anything, not one tiny little thing?"

I shake my head.

"Have you gone through your mother's things yet?"

"My mother's things?"

"Her clothes, jewelry, possessions. Did somebody already box them up?"

"No." I don't tell him that Tata practically turned his bedroom into a shrine to my mother.

"Maybe you should try that. See if it helps. We'll talk next week. Oh, Isabel, I almost forgot."

"What?"

"Frank sends you a message. He says when you visit him next week, bring the ukulele."

Thief

It's Sunday night and I still haven't gotten up enough nerve to ask Tata for the ukulele. He keeps it on the dresser next to their wedding picture and the tiara.

I decide to take it without permission. Tata might say no and I won't visit Frank without it.

When Auntie Bernadette honks the horn twice for Olivia and me, I grab the ukulele case and dash out the door.

No Punishment

"Did you search through your mother's things?" Ed asks.

I think about lying because I don't want anything to keep me away from my visit with Frank. Instead I stare at the ukulele case and shake my head.

Ed laces his fingers together and taps his knuckles, looking at me for a long moment. He stretches out on the couch, flat on his back, and stares at the ceiling.

"Isabel, what do you do with your day?"

"I go to school."

"After school. Do you have any hobbies?"

"I watch the store."

"Until you go to bed?"

"Until supper."

"Do you have to cook supper every night?"

"Auntie makes it most nights. She cooks it at her house and brings it to us. Or sometimes she fixes dinner at our home."

"After supper, what do you do?"

"I wash dishes, then I sometimes watch TV or read."

"Reading is good. Do you have any other special hobbies? Like sports?"

"I'm not good at sports. Except maybe . . ."

"Maybe what?"

"Well, I like to dive, but I don't know if I'm good at it."

"Diving. Hmmm . . . scuba diving?"

"No, diving off diving boards." Suddenly it sounds kind of stupid and I don't even know why I said it.

"Are there diving teams here that you can join?" Ed asks.

"Oh, I don't know. The university has a team, but that's for college students. Do I get to see Frank today?"

"Yes, of course. I told you that you would. Did you think I'd change my mind?"

"I guess because . . . I didn't look at my mother's things."

"Isabel, I can only make suggestions. You have to do the work. Besides, I'm not here to punish you. I'm here to help."

Doesn't Ed realize that Frank is the one who needs the help?

Frank's Hospital Room

White
windowless
two beds
two boys
too many scars.

First Visit

I try not to stare at Frank's roommate. Shiny pink patches and red scars cover his face.

Ed tells Frank he should have told him that he had two pretty sisters. Frank doesn't smile, but there's something different about him in his eyes. Even though he won't look at me for very long, he seems like he's really here, out of the trance.

Ed takes Frank's roommate for a walk while Frank and I visit. He props the door open before they walk away.

"I brought the ukulele," I say, holding out the case.

"Thanks." He doesn't reach for it, so I put it down on the floor.

I'm standing, arms folded, the case at my feet, speechless. I try to think of something to say, but I can't think of one word.

"Sit down," he says. Frank is sitting at the foot of his bed, so I settle close to the headboard. Finally, I think of something.

"I'm sorry Tata hasn't come by." Of all the words to be taking a spin inside my head.

"He has. He comes every day."

"He does?"

"In the afternoon. He never stays long. Never talks about anything except fishing."

Maybe Frank didn't ask Tata for the ukulele because he was afraid what the answer might be.

"Are they nice to you in here?"

"Yeah, but the food stinks."

"Sorry."

He scowls. "Why are you sorry? You didn't make it."

I stare at the other bed. "Do you like your roommate?"

"He's okay. He picks his nose, though."

"Yuck."

"He thinks I don't see him, but I do. I don't shake his hand or anything."

I can't help but smile. "What's wrong with his face?"

"He likes to play with matches."

Frank scratches his toe. I feel so strange in this room with my brother. I want to blink and make him little again, as little as Mary Kelly's baby brother. I'd watch him real careful this time and keep him from turning into a boy who has to stay in a white room with a weird stranger and eat food that stinks.

Missing: One Ukulele

Tata waits for us in the kitchen. I'm hoping he wants to ask about our visit with Frank, but he says, "We've been robbed."

I look around the room. Everything is in place. Though there isn't anything in here worth taking.

"Someone stole your mother's ukulele."

I don't hesitate. "I took it to Frank."

The vein on his temple bulges and he stares a hole through me. I stare back. "Why?" he asks. "You know that's not yours."

"Frank wanted it. And no one's using it. What's the big deal?"

Tata tells my sister, "Go play, Olivia."

"I have homework," she says.

"Go play."

She marches out of the room, leaving me to face Tata alone. He waits until he hears our bedroom door slam. "You're being disrespectful, Isabel."

"You're not being fair. Frank used to be happy when he played. Why don't you want him to be happy?"

"I don't have to explain anything. I'm your father."

My breaths come short and fast. My head pounds.

"Why didn't you know about the words on Frank's wall? Maybe if you asked Frank to go fishing instead of Roman, Frank would be here now, not in that hospital. Why don't you care?" I'm yelling and it doesn't matter if anyone can hear me. Everyone in Malesso can think I'm a disrespectful daughter. I want to empty the words that have been building inside of me.

Tata stares at me like he's never seen me before.

I leave the house. I don't run, though. I walk, my chin up, my heart pounding, my head clear.

Exposed

When I reach the pier, Mrs. Cruz is packing up her pictures and her folding chair. "Isabel, you arrived just in time. Would you mind helping me take my stuff home?"

"Sure." I'm not in any hurry to return to my house.

"John Wayne usually helps me, but he's spear fishing with Roman. Did you see the boots Roman bought John Wayne?"

I nod.

"He bought his mother a freezer, too. I don't think he's bought himself a thing with any of the prize money. What a respectful young man!"

I carry the chair and giant umbrella while Mrs. Cruz carries her pictures. It doesn't take long to reach her beachside house. At the front door she says, "Just put the chair and umbrella down here. I'll have to drag it out tomorrow. How's Frank?"

"He's better. I saw him today."

"Tell him hello. Maybe John Wayne and I can visit him."

"They're kind of picky about visitors."

"Oh," she says, staring down at her feet.

I'm not sure she understands, so I add, "I mean I just got to see him today for the first time."

"Well, please, let him know we asked about him. Thanks for your help, Isabel."

She starts to close the door and I quickly blurt out, "Mrs. Cruz, can I see the picture you painted of my mother?"

Mrs. Cruz leads me to her sunroom, where she paints. The room practically touches the ocean's edge. The ocean is so close, I feel like I'm on a boat instead of inside a house.

"I didn't want to mention the picture again," Mrs. Cruz says. "I thought I might be acting too pushy. I think I did a pretty good job. Your mother was so beautiful. It's easy to paint beautiful people. It's the ugly ones that are difficult. I have to search and search for something good to focus on."

The room is messy with paints and easels with half-finished pictures of fish. Three nude paintings hang on the wall and I feel the blood rush from my head as I try to brace myself for what I'm about to see.

Mrs. Cruz waddles to the north wall, then browses through several canvases leaning against one another like fallen dominos.

"Ah, here it is." She turns the canvas around, holding it out in front of her so that I can get a good look.

To my relief, my mother isn't nude, but wearing a full-length white nightgown. Her long black hair flows over her left shoulder and touches the ground. She's not the mother I've seen in the pictures I've studied around our house. She's not the laughing little girl eating a mango, the smiling fiesta queen, the shy bride, or even the peaceful mother holding Frank when he was a baby and I was at her knee. She's sad. Sad and beautiful. The mother I remember.

Focal Point

I carry the picture home and find a place for it on the living-room wall over the TV, not bothering to ask Tata's permission. He's drinking a Miller Lite in his chair while he watches me pound a nail into the wall. When I'm finished, he stands and walks to the picture. His chest jumps and he makes what sounds like a hiccup. He runs a finger down my mother's hair, then hides his face in his hands. "Erlinda," he whispers.

I can't tell if it's the beer that causes his tears or the picture, but I don't care. I hug my father and he does something he hasn't done since my mother died. He hugs me back.

Sleep

Olivia hasn't had a nightmare in a couple of weeks. Every night has been a dry one for her, too, even without trips to the bathroom. Tonight, I close my eyes and before long I'm dreaming of the Fragrant Lady.

Like before, I catch a glimpse of her wearing a flowing white gown and like before, I follow her and the sweet scent to the ocean. But this time when she turns around and waves, I see her face. It's my mother's.

Expectations

As usual, Tata has already left for the sea. I can't help but feel a little disappointed. Somehow I'd hoped that he'd have breakfast with us this morning. I try not to check where he slept, but the bed is still untouched and he's left his pillow on the floor.

When I open my notebook to write today's list, I notice these words in my father's handwriting:

I care.

Open

After school, I go to my parents' room and open the bottom drawer, where I know my mother kept special memories. I know that because every year she opened it and dragged out her blue fiesta queen dress. Today I find out what else is in there. I discover a tiny box that holds baby teeth. Seeing them makes me think of when I lost my first one. Tata had said, "Put your tooth under the pillow and the tooth fairy will leave you a quarter."

Then my mother said, "Oh, I've heard the tooth fairy leaves five dollars now." Tata choked on his sandwich. He coughed while Mom laughed. In the morning I had five dollars waiting under my pillow.

There's a locket on a thin chain that's worked its way into a tangled ball at one corner of the drawer. Inside the locket is a picture of my grandmother and grandfather. They died before I was born.

At the bottom of the drawer is a stack of stories tied with a yellow ribbon. At first I think they're Olivia's because the handwriting is big and awkward. Then I see my name spelled out, but the s is backward. I even remember one of the stories. It was about a wild pig that lived in the jungle, probably the beginning of the pig stories I tell Olivia. I got a C+ on it, which for some reason makes me mad. It was a good story. And I was only a little kid. That should count for something. But now the thought of my mother saving it, tying a yellow ribbon around the story like it was special to her, makes my insides tumble.

I don't know why my mother left us, why she stopped playing silly songs on the ukulele, laughing at Frank's stupid knock-knock jokes, why she stopped dancing with my father. But now finding all these things in her drawer of treasures, I do know that no matter how much sorrow filled my mother, she loved me. This I know for sure.

Sober

All week I'm filled with happy memories of my mother. Then today I remember dark and painful moments.

Remember the drives to St. Cletus School, Mom? I prayed to every saint while you speeded, our car hugging the edge of the road that winds up the cliff toward Talofofo.

You spoke quickly, naming all the items you needed to order from the vendors: toilet paper, apples, eggs, milk, potatoes, Chee-tos, and Spam . . . "Damn Spam," you said, laughing like it was funny. Repeating the words, saying them so fast that I prayed the groceries would fall down straight from heaven. Then maybe you'd slow down.

Remember when you did slow down, Mom? Remember the days you made our breakfast, then crawled back into bed and Auntie had to drive us to school?

Remember when Frank almost drowned and you didn't come out of your room, not even when Auntie told you what happened? You acted like Frank had died.

Remember how you let me hold Olivia when she was a very tiny baby because you said her crying gave you a headache?

Remember how I had to stand on my tippy toes to get her diapers? And you told me to go ahead and change her? "Just this time," you said. But then it was the next time, too.

Say His Name

Frank has been in the hospital for three weeks. Still no one mentions him at school. Not Sister Agnes or Sister Rachel. Not Delia, Tonya, or Mary Kelly. It reminds me of the days after my mother died. I want to shout, *My brother is alive. Say his name.* If someone would just say "Frank" once, then maybe I could start to believe that he was going to be okay.

A True Love Story

On the way to the hospital, I tell Auntie, "Did you know that Tata visits Frank every day?"

"Yes," Auntie says.

"But why won't he meet with Ed?"

"Pride. A lot of Chamorro men think it's a sign of weakness to admit they need help. That's why most of my customers are women. A little pride is okay, but some Chamorro men have too much. Not Fernando. That's why I married him."

I must have been right about my uncle marrying my auntie because she was a *suruhana*. So even though I know, I ask, "He lets you help him?"

"Yes, exactly. And he helped me, too."

"What do you mean?" I ask.

"I was twenty-five when I met Fernando. It was at the fiesta in Umatac. My cousin Celia and I went together. Celia was beautiful and when the music played, men raced over to ask her to dance. The one that reached Celia first won her as a partner. The others asked the remaining girls. Except for me. I hadn't danced since school, when I would cha-cha with my girlhood friends on the playground."

I can't picture Auntie dancing at all, but now I ache at the thought of her sitting against the wall while everyone else danced.

Auntie misses our turn to the road leading to the hospital and has to make a right at the next street, then backtrack. She always messes up when she's telling a story. Usually I get impatient because I can't stand being late, but today I don't care. I want to hear the rest.

"Was Uncle Fernando there?" Olivia asks.

Auntie smiles. "Yes. Fernando was across the room, staring at me. I'd noticed him earlier because of his fine square jaw. He walked toward me, passing Celia and the other pretty dancing girls. He introduced himself, held out his arm, and said, 'Let's dance.'

"I looked down at my bad hand and said, 'I haven't done the cha-cha in years. I'll make a terrible dance partner.' But he stood there with his arm out until I agreed to join him. And you know what, Olivia?"

"What?" she asks.

"I wasn't bad. In fact, Fernando was such a great

dancer, he made me look like one, too. Somehow my feet remembered those playground steps. Fernando's eyes never left mine and we've been dancing through life together ever since."

Olivia scrunches her face. "But Uncle Fernando doesn't dance—he just sleeps."

"That's not what she meant, Olivia," I say. But how do you explain true love to a seven-year-old?

I've known Auntie and Uncle Fernando my entire life, but today I feel like we've just met. The next time I see Uncle Fernando, I'm going to check out that fine square jaw.

Good

Ed is eating fried chicken today instead of a Big Mac. He opens a towelette and wipes his fingers before shaking my hand.

"Isabel, I have some good news. My friend has a cousin who is a swim coach at the university. They have an opening on their junior team. He said you could try out."

"But I'm not that good. I've just dived a few times."

"Let's let him decide, okay? Tryouts begin at nine. Maybe your father can take you Saturday."

"I doubt that." He'd be too busy fishing.

Ed pauses like he's about to ask why. Then says, "Or maybe your auntie?"

"Maybe."

My stomach rumbles. I wish Ed would mind his own business.

"Isabel, you've taken on a lot of responsibility since your mother died and I suspect since before she died, too. You need to have something of your own that has nothing to do with taking care of your family. Maybe it's the diving."

"But I've never had lessons."

"Maybe it's not diving. But it's got to be something. By the way, Frank is playing the ukulele. He's great."

I nod. "My mother was great, too. She taught Frank."

Ed smiles. "So you remember?"

I know this is what he's wanted from me since our first meeting and even though I swore I'd never discuss my mother with him, today I want to. "I started remembering last week."

"Good."

"But I'm starting to remember bad things, too."

"Good."

Confused, I squint. "Good?"

"You need to remember the good *and* bad."

"I still can't figure out why she killed . . . herself."

I choke back a lump in my throat.

"You probably never will. That's the sad part. Most survivors don't ever know why. But you can learn something from what your mother did."

I take a big breath. "What?"

Ed gets up and moves to the chair directly across from me. "That no matter how bad life gets, no matter how sad, there is always another way. There are people to help. We live on a tiny island in a big ocean. When we're depressed, it's sometimes easy to forget how big the ocean is, how big life is." He pauses, leaning forward. "Maybe your mother forgot how big the ocean was. Someone could have helped if she would have let them."

I think about what Ed told me as we leave his office and head to Frank's room on the other wing. My mind is dizzy with thoughts of Frank and his scars, Olivia's nightmares, Auntie's guilt, and Tata's loneliness. I think about the space my mother left that I must now fill. My mother's death hurt so many people. Didn't she think about us before she died? I feel so angry that I want to scream. If a pool was in front of me, I'd dive right in. But I would come back up for air.

Growing

Frank is in the TV room, watching *Batman* reruns with some of the other patients. "Hey," he says when he sees me. "Let's go to my room."

I follow him as he shuffles down the hall, wearing shorts, a T-shirt, and slippers. He seems taller, lankier, older. When did that happen? Inside his room, I try to steal a glimpse at the scars on his arm, but he catches me.

"Knock, knock," he says.

The words startle me, but I say, "Who's there?"

"Hat."

"Hat who?"

He holds out his arm for me to see, pointing to the words. "See, Isabel, *I h-a-t. I hat.*" Then he points to me and says, "You shoe."

It's not even funny, but I want it to be. I *really* want it to be.

Matthew Kolby Johnson

Auntie and I visit Mary Kelly's baby brother at their house. I forgot to buy a gift, but Auntie Bernadette gives him a photo album that she says is from both of us.

"You'll have to come to my baby fiesta," Auntie says. "It's in a couple of weeks."

Mary Kelly hands Matthew over to Auntie. "I told Mom we should call him Bernie after you since you knew he was going to be a boy."

"Oh, I don't much care for my name. Erlinda didn't like hers either. Our mother wasn't good at names." Matthew looks like an ugly little old man, almost completely bald and red-faced. I can't help but think how Chamorro babies are prettier, with their dark skin and jet black hair. When he burps, he spits up white goo and it dribbles down his chin.

"Isn't he beautiful?" Mary Kelly asks.

"Oh, yes," we lie.

While Mary Kelly shows Auntie the pink nursery, Mrs. Johnson leans over and touches my hand. "How are you, Isabel?"

"I'm fine," I say, and without thinking about it, I add, "I'm going to try out for the junior diving team."

List to Prepare for
Diving Team Tryouts

1. Call Auntie and ask her to take me to the university for diving tryouts
2. Friday remind her that I need to be there by nine
3. Ask Mrs. Cruz if she will watch Olivia and the store Saturday morning
4. Close my eyes
5. Imagine the water
6. See me doing a perfect dive
7. Repeat numbers 4, 5, and 6 again and again

Tryouts

Saturday morning, I'm a nervous wreck. My stomach is in knots, my bathing suit smells sour, and I have my first pimple. Auntie is late picking me up for the tryouts. She said she'd pick me up at eight-thirty sharp and it's already five minutes after. I look out the window, bouncing on my heels. "Hurry, Auntie," I mutter.

Tata comes into the living room, wearing a clean striped shirt, the one he used to wear to Mass. "Ready?"

I swallow. I hadn't bothered to tell him about the tryouts. I figured he'd be fishing.

"Ready?" Tata asks again.

"Sure." I grab my towel and follow him out the door.

Plunge

The university pool is huge, bigger than I remembered, and I'm not the only one trying out. Five other people about my age are sitting on a bench, waiting. My stomach tumbles.

The highest diving board is twice as tall as the base pool's. But the coach tells me it's okay if I dive off the lower one. "I'm just observing your technique today."

Technique? Did Ed tell him that I had a technique?

I consider choosing the highest diving board to impress the coach, but a picture of my body changing into a pretzel in midair flashes in my mind. I go over to the lower one, trying to forget about how this is an audition, one that suddenly seems so important to me.

As I climb up the ladder I tell myself it's okay if I don't do well. I'll go back to the way things were. But I realize now I don't want to go back. I want something new and—like Ed says—something of my own.

I raise my arms above my head, then bend at the waist, aiming toward the water. I lean forward and without hesitating I jump and dive in. I don't even think about the coach or Tata watching. I let the magic of the motion happen and when I get out of the water, the coach says, "Can you do that again?"

Repeat, Please

Again and again, I dive for the coach. Each time I finish, he nods and says, "Nice. Once more, please."

Finally he hands me a towel. "Isabel, we'll try to let you know tonight. Can I get your phone number?"

Tata rattles off the number before I can answer. His voice shakes, and I wonder if I've embarrassed him. It seems like I dived a lot better that day at the base pool.

On the way home, Tata tells me, "Your great-uncle was an excellent diver. Only, he dove off some of the cliffs around the island. People gathered in big crowds to see him. He was really something."

"Oh," I say, wishing Auntie had brought me to the audition. I knew I'd be a big disappointment to him.

Tata stares straight ahead at the road and smiles. "You must have gotten your talent from him."

Boiling Water

"Waiting for the phone to ring is like waiting for a pot of water to boil," Auntie tells me.

"I'm not waiting. I'm reading."

"You should go with us."

How do I tell Auntie that I won't hear Father David say Mass? My mind will be on the call.

"The coach may not be phoning you because he's at Mass."

"Good-bye, Auntie."

She leaves with Olivia and Tata, too. My father hasn't been to church since my mother's funeral. Maybe he goes because he doesn't want to make me nervous. After the door shuts, Tata opens it and sticks his head in. "I don't think you have anything to worry about." He winks before closing the door.

His words warm me, but now I want to make the diving team more than anything. I want to make it for me and for my family.

The words in my book blur together and I read the same page eight times. I turn on the TV, but there's nothing worth watching. I think of calling Teresita, but she'll be at Mass. And Mary Kelly will be at the base chapel. Besides, I don't want to hear any more about her baby brother.

At eight I know that Mass has ended and my family will return soon to find I haven't learned anything. But the phone rings before they arrive.

"Hello?"

"Isabel Moreno, please."

"Speaking."

"Isabel, this is Coach Alonzo. Welcome to the team."

A Chance

The coach says I have a lot to learn, but he thinks I have talent and potential. "You'll be an alternate diver. That means you'll practice with the team, but you'll only compete when one of the other divers can't. Next year, we'll reassess how you've progressed. Are you willing to work under those conditions?"

"Yes, thank you, Coach."

"You might not be thanking me at the end of next week. We practice six days a week, including Saturdays."

Something stabs me in the pit of my stomach.

The store. Who will tend to the store?

"I'll have to get back with you after I talk to my father."

"Good enough. Let me know as soon as possible. By the way, Isabel, your great focus convinced me that you belong on the team."

Fly

Tata hired Mrs. Cruz to work at the store every afternoon and Saturday mornings so that I can attend diving practice. He said it was okay if she sold her pictures there, too, as long as the subjects had fins or wore clothes.

I feel like I've grown wings and can fly. I want to soar through the sky and tell everyone my good news—Teresita, Roman, Delia and Tonya, Mary Kelly and Mrs. Johnson. But I decide to wait until Monday night, because more than anything on this earth, I want Frank to be the next person to know.

Growing Up

Tonight, Olivia tells me that she's growing up. "I'll be eight next week," she reminds me.

I almost forgot. Our lives have been so busy these days.

"Tata says I can have a slumber party. We can pull our beds apart."

Olivia doesn't have to tell me that the reason she wants the beds apart is because she doesn't want her friends to think she's a baby.

I walk over to the bed. "We can do it right now."

Her face looks panicked. "Wait," she says. "Can we keep them together for one more night?"

I smile, happy that there's still a part of her that doesn't want to grow up. "Sure."

And tonight I hold my baby sister tight and tell her a story about a pig that moves to Hollywood and becomes a famous movie star.

Golai Hagun Sune

28 taro leaves*
7 cups of water
1½ cups of grated coconut
4 tablespoons of lime juice
1½ tablespoons of grated ginger
Salt to taste
2 cloves of garlic, minced
1 large onion, chopped
1½ cups of diluted coconut milk
2 big dashes of Tabasco sauce

Chop taro leaves and boil in water for one hour. Drain leaves and add grated coconut, lime juice, ginger, salt, garlic, and onion. Boil for another four minutes. Add the diluted coconut milk and Tabasco sauce. Remove from stove. Serve with rice.

*Fresh spinach leaves may be substituted for taro leaves.

The Gift

*O*utside the kitchen the taro leaves have grown thick, probably too thick to be tasty. I open the drawer next to the sink and pull out the sharpest knife. It's the knife my mother used to make her *golai hagun sune,* the same one I hid from my brother a month ago.

I pass over the oldest leaves with the curly edges, choosing the fresh young ones. Before I finish cutting the first stem, I remember an old Chamorro song my mother hummed often and the tune finds its way to my lips.

My father shakes the net by the cabana and a coconut escapes to the ground. With his machete, Tata cuts the husk in half with one clean whack. When my mother made the dish, he'd look up at her, pretending like he was going to chop the coconut in a million pieces. But of course he didn't. Then he laughed and hugged her.

Today he works quietly as he carefully pulls the husk away. He takes the round shell from the center and makes a hole before draining the milk into the yellow bowl.

After I chop the onions, Tata and I take turns grating the coconut until our fingers feel raw. But the pain doesn't bother us much. Tomorrow at the baby fiesta, Auntie's guests will have some *golai hagun sune* and Monday, Frank will eat some of his favorite dish. I can hardly wait to see their faces when they discover the dish we made. I won't even let it bother me when Auntie says something like, "See, Isabel, I'll make a *suruhana* of you after all." For I know that making my mother's best recipe has nothing to do with becoming a healer, but everything to do with love.

Tata sings. I sing. Our voices become one. I remember when I was a little girl, sitting in the kitchen, watching my mother from my book, wondering, Why the fuss? Why go through this much trouble to make such a dish?

Now I know why.

Author's Note

I spent my fifth- and sixth-grade years on Guam. Those two years proved magical. Coconuts and hibiscus grew in our yard. We swam and snorkeled all year long. I attended fiestas, explored caves, experienced typhoons and earthquakes.

Best of all, I learned what it was like to live among people of a different culture because each weekday the school bus drove me to P. C. Lujan Elementary School, where I attended classes with Chamorro and with other military kids.

Two years ago the Guam Council of the International Reading Association invited me back to visit schools. When I returned to P. C. Lujan, I discovered my sixth-grade classroom was now the library. It was a tender moment. Life sometimes does make a complete circle.

About the Author

Kimberly Willis Holt is the author of many award-winning novels, including *When Zachary Beaver Came to Town*, *My Louisiana Sky*, *Keeper of the Night*, *Part of Me*, *The Water Seeker*, and the Piper Reed series.

Having lived all over the world, including Guam, Ms. Holt now resides in Texas with her family.

GOFISH

questions for the author

KIMBERLY WILLIS HOLT

Shannon Holt

You spent time in Guam as a child. What was the inspiration for this particular story?
When I returned as an adult to visit the schools on Guam, I learned that a former classmate had committed suicide the prior year. A mutual friend told me that she'd died praying on her knees. I couldn't shake that image. And it was that image that led me to Isabel's story. At first, I thought her story was going to be one among several in a short-story collection. But as I wrote I had to know that she would be okay. That required the space of a novel.

Why did you decide to tell this story through short passages?
I've always loved the idea of writing a book with short chapters. However, in the past when I've tried to do so, it seemed forced. With *Keeper of the Night*, the spare form came naturally. It was a refreshing departure for me, and that in itself was rewarding. Part of the satisfaction I get as a writer is knowing I can explore different ways to tell a story. As far as difficulties are concerned, I encountered the same challenges I do when I write in a more traditional form. Did I tell the story well enough? Do the characters have depth?

Do you have a favorite passage?
Usually my favorite passages are not my readers' favorites.
In *Keeper* there is a chapter where Isabel's father takes her
to the diving team tryouts. Later he tells her about her uncle
who was a great diver. Isabel thinks that is her father's way
of telling her she wasn't that great. Then her father says,
"You must have gotten your talent from him." That part still
chokes me up, because no matter how old I am, I want my
parents to be proud of me. It's funny, one of my sisters said
that's the part that got to her the most.

I was most intimidated to write about Frank being found
after he cut himself. I dreaded writing that scene. I didn't
want it to be melodramatic. So I chose to write it in short
clips, like a photographer taking fast snapshots of an event.
Originally, I did it that way just to get some words down,
thinking that I'd go back to it. Ultimately, I chose to leave it as
it was.

**Many of the scenes and people in the book feel very
detailed and authentic. Do you write from real-life
observations?**
My writing is like making gumbo—a little of this, a little of
that mixed together. Some of those people were inspired by
bits of people whom I met on the island; many details I
made up. The oddest thing is, after spending so much time
with the story, I couldn't tell you what is true and what isn't. I
like to think the best fiction becomes its own truth.

**You thank many people in your acknowledgments.
What kind of preparation did you do to write this book?**
Six months after the trip to Guam during which I visited the
schools, I had to return to do research. I spoke to many people on
the island, spent time in the library, and tried to soak up the
setting. Later, I depended greatly on several people for answers

via e-mail. Because suicide and self-mutilation were part of the story, I interviewed the director of the suicide crisis center in Amarillo, Texas, as well as making contact with a Guam crisis center counselor.

Do you like to get a lot of feedback as you write?
My daughter is the only person allowed to read (or I should say hear) my first drafts. I try not to let anyone else read anything earlier than the seventh draft. The reason is that I'm still figuring out the story and the characters in early drafts. I don't want other people to influence me at that organic stage.

How long does it take you to write a book?
I'll give the answer that I heard Bruce Coville give: all my life. Technically, it takes about one year to two years, but how can you discount a writer's entire life experience? That is truly a part of every story.

Any advice for writers who have great story ideas but just can't seem to get them down on paper?
If you are meant to be a writer, you will put it down on paper even if it means you have to write a lousy first draft. If not, maybe you aren't meant to write that story. Or maybe it's not the right time to write that story. Or maybe you are meant to do something else.

As a writer, what is your greatest fear?
Boring the reader.

Isabel must grow up fast in this story and seems exceptionally mature for her age. Why did you want to tell the story from her perspective?
Isabel is a firstborn child, as am I. But I didn't choose to tell it from her point of view. She chose me.

In response to a loved one's suicide, are there typical stages a person goes through?
I'm certainly not an expert on this subject, but my research, which included talking to survivors of suicide, indicated that the stages that Isabel goes through are typical. The sadness, the anger, the trying to figure out why it happened. One thing the suicide crisis director told me was that the survivor has to find something of her own to help her get on with living. For Isabel, that is the diving.

What is your response to stress?
I'm afraid I'm not good at handling stress. Thank goodness, I married someone who is. Although I do think I am good at handling big difficulties. It's the small ones that I find most challenging. I guess you could say I sweat the small stuff.

Are you a list maker like Isabel?
Yes, I feel most secure with my lists. This drove my mother crazy because my dad was a list maker too. And he even made lists for her.

One theme that emerges from the book has to do with asking for (or not knowing how to ask for) help from other people. Why does Isabel struggle alone until the last part of the book?
I believe it's because she is a firstborn and thinks it is a weakness to ask for help. Tata's neglecting to deal with his wife's death plays a huge role in this family's lack of communication. One thing the crisis counselor from Guam told me was that when a Chamorro wife dies, the father goes on with his life and the grandmother or auntie steps in and tries to fill the mother's role. The counselor said Guam was very much a matriarchal society.

Isabel is very much afraid to let the bucket of her emotions spill over. What do you think she fears will happen?
Tata is not holding the family together. Isabel feels that someone must, and that someone is her. I think Isabel believes she must stay strong, and that means not releasing her emotions.

What do you like best about being a writer?
I get to wear my pajamas to work.

Chapter One

Nothing ever happens in Antler, Texas. Nothing much at all. Until this afternoon, when an old blue Thunderbird pulls a trailer decorated with Christmas lights into the Dairy Maid parking lot. The red words painted on the trailer cause quite a buzz around town, and before an hour is up, half of Antler is standing in line with two dollars clutched in hand to see the fattest boy in the world.

Since it's too late in the summer for firecrackers and too early for the Ladybug Waltz, Cal and I join Miss Myrtie Mae and the First Baptist Quilting Bee at the back of the line.

Miss Myrtie Mae wears a wide-brimmed straw hat. She claims that she's never exposed her skin to sun. Even so, wrinkles fold into her face like an unironed shirt. She takes her job as town historian and librarian seriously, and as usual, her camera hangs around her neck. "Toby, how's your mom?"

"Fine," I say.

"That will really be something if she wins."

"Yes, ma'am, it will." My mouth says the words, but my mind is not wanting to settle on a picture of her winning. Mom dreams of following in the footsteps of her favorite singer, Tammy Wynette. Last month she entered a singing contest in Amarillo and won first place. She got a trophy and an all-expense-paid trip to Nashville for a week to enter the National Amateurs' Country Music Competition at the Grand Ole Opry. The winner gets to cut a record album.

Cars and pickups pull into the Dairy Maid parking lot. Some people make no bones about it. They just get in line to see him. Others try to act like they don't know anything about the buzz. They enter the Dairy Maid, place their orders, and exit with Coke floats, chocolate-dipped cones, or curlicue fries, then wander to the back of the line. They don't fool me.

The line isn't moving because the big event hasn't started. Some skinny guy wearing a tuxedo, smoking a pipe, is taking the money and giving out green tickets. Cal could stand in line forever to relieve his curiosity, He knows more gossip than any old biddy in Antler because he gathers it down at the cotton gin, where his dad and the other farmers drink coffee.

"I got better things to do than this," I tell Cal. Like eat. My stomach's been growling all the time now because I haven't had a decent meal since Mom left a few days ago. Not that she cooked much lately since she was getting ready for that stupid contest. But I miss the fried catfish and barbecue dinners she brought home from the Bowl-a-Rama Cafe, where she works.

"Oh, come on, Toby," Cal begs. "He'll probably move out tomorrow and we'll never get another chance."

"He's just some fat kid. Heck, Malcolm Clifton probably has him beat hands down." Malcolm's mom claims he's big boned, not fat, but we've seen him pack away six jumbo burgers. I sigh real big like my dad does when he looks at my report card filled with Cs. "Okay," I say. "But I'm only waiting ten more minutes. After that, I'm splitting."

Cal grins that stupid grin with his black tooth showing. He likes to brag that he got his black tooth playing football, but I know the real story. His sister, Kate, socked him good when he scratched up her Carole King album. Cal says he was sick of hearing "You Make Me Feel Like a Natural Woman" every stinking day of his life.

Scarlett Stalling walks toward the line, holding her bratty sister Tara's hand. Scarlett looks cool wearing a bikini top underneath an open white blouse and hip huggers that hit right below her belly button. With her golden tan and long, silky blond hair, she could do a commercial for Coppertone.

Scarlett doesn't go to the back of the line. She walks over to me. *To me.* Smiling, flashing that Ultra Brite sex appeal smile and the tiny gap between her two front teeth. Cal grins, giving her the tooth, but I lower my eyelids half-mast and jerk my head back a little as if to say, "Hey."

Then she speaks. "Hey, Toby, would ya'll do me a favor?"

"Sure," I squeak, killing my cool act in one split second.

Scarlett flutters her eyelashes, and I suck in my breath. "Take Tara in for me." She passes her little sister's sticky hand like she's handing over a dog's leash. Then she squeezes her fingers into her pocket and pulls out two crumpled dollar bills. I would give anything to be one of those lucky dollar bills tucked into her pocket.

She flips back her blond mane. "I've got to get back home and get ready. Juan's dropping by soon."

The skin on my chest prickles. Mom is right. Scarlett Stalling is a flirt. Mom always told me, "You better stay a spittin' distance from that girl. Her mother had a bad reputation when I went to school, and the apple doesn't fall far from the tree."

Cal punches my shoulder. "Great going, ladies' man!"

I watch Scarlett's tight jeans sway toward her house so she can get ready for the only Mexican guy in Antler Junior High. Juan already shaves. He's a head taller than the rest of the guys (two heads taller than me). That gives him an instant ticket to play first string on our basketball team, even though he's slow footed and a lousy shot. Whenever I see him around town, a number-five-iron golf club swings at his side. I don't plan to ever give him a reason to use it.

"Fatty, fatty, two by four," Tara chimes as she stares at the trailer. "Can't get through the kitchen door."

"Shut up, squirt," I mutter.

Miss Myrtie Mae frowns at me.

Tara yanks on my arm. "Uummmm!" she hollers. "You said shut up. Scarlett!" She rises on her toes as if that makes her louder. "Toby said shut up to me!"

But it's too late. Scarlett has already disappeared across the street. She's probably home smearing gloss on those pouty lips while I hold her whiny sister's lollipop fingers, standing next to my black-toothed best friend, waiting to see the fattest boy in the world.

Some summers change you forever.
Toby's mom leaves. His best friend's brother
is away at war. And then Zachary Beaver,
the fattest boy in the world, shows up.

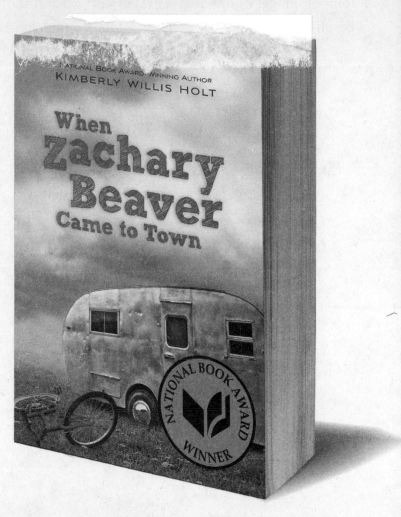

Turn the page to read an excerpt from

When Zachary Beaver Came to Town

by Kimberly Willis Holt.